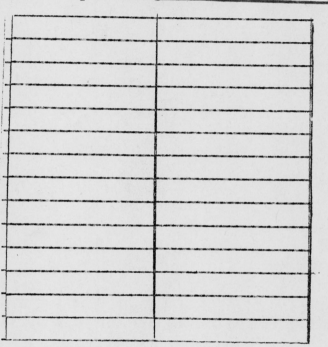

THE GIRL FROM ADDIS

Ted Allbeury

THE GIRL FROM ADDIS

GRANADA
London Toronto Sydney New York

Granada Publishing Limited
8 Grafton Street London W1X 3LA

Published by Granada Publishing 1984

British Library Cataloguing in Publication Data
Allbeury, Ted
  The girl from Addis.
  I. Title
  823'.914[F]   PR6051.L52

ISBN 0 246 11856 3

Printed in Great Britain by
Billing and Sons Limited,
London and Worcester

As the man who once ran the pirate radio station known as Radio 390 I am unlikely to be accused of seeing BBC Radio through rose-tinted glasses. So let me say that I feel that BBC Radio is the most valuable cultural institution that this country has. Its professional standards, both technically and in its ethos, are the envy of the rest of the world.

BBC Radio has one other virtue – it is much loved and appreciated by its home audience. Because I am a writer I have more experience of the BBC's Radio Drama department than its other sections. Their help to new writers, and their awesome technical expertise are less well-known than the hours of entertainment that they provide. So this book is dedicated to all those men and women, past and present, of BBC Drama, who have entertained us all so well. Long may they go on doing so – this book is for them – with love.

Ted Allbeury
July '83

1

We were an hour out of Cairo and there was no touch-down before Addis. In the old days we should have had to stop at Khartoum at least. Probably Wadi Halfa as well. As the thermals came up from the baked sand the aircraft dropped, a hundred feet at a time, and then surged up again. Passengers pressed their feet to the floor in panic reflexes, and silently cursed the pilot. It lasted for fifteen minutes and then we were at cruising height. It was going to be a long flight so I lay across the three seats and got out the paperback I'd bought at Heathrow. But I couldn't settle.

It seemed like a dream, or maybe a nightmare, to be going back to Ethiopia after all those years. There was a decade when you could use the end of the war as a bench-mark for measuring time. It had been 1942 when I left Addis. I'd been given forty-eight hours to get out and it hadn't been easy to hand over.

MI6 sent me in as soon as we had liberated the country in 1941 and the Emperor had gone back. My official appoint-ment was as Military Liaison Officer to His Imperial Highness. It took them nearly a year to rumble me, and the first I'd known that my cover had gone was after a reception for the Greek Ambassador at the Palace. The colonel of the Imperial Guard had escorted me across the parade ground and casually suggested that we have a look at the new stables. In the first one was Mamu. He was from Harar, about fifteen years old. He lay on some filthy straw and Colonel Mulugueta pointed at Mamu's feet with his stick. The bones that stuck through the flesh were a beautiful dazzling white and despite his black skin the raw red meat where they'd smashed at him, was an even darker red. There was not much blood but that was probably because he'd been dead for some days. Mamu was my houseboy. He'd been missing for two weeks.

Mulugueta's smoky eyes had watched me carefully as I read the note he handed to me. It was signed by His Imperial Highness and was in French. I was *persona non grata* and I'd got forty-eight hours to get out.

I phoned our embassy. They didn't want to know. But they condescended to radio Nairobi and Cairo. The Third Secretary brought round the answer a couple of hours later. My replacement would be flown over from Aden that night and I was to hand over to him at Kathi Kathikis's night-club. Any time after eleven. The same plane would take me on to Nairobi.

There was only one thing in Addis that London really cared about at that time and that was the Jonnet business. Jonnet was a merchant with bases all over that neck of the woods. Asmara, Addis, Dire Dawa, Mogadishu, Aden and the Yemen. He was an Armenian and a millionaire several times over. He had influence at all levels everywhere, with the Italians, the Vichy French, the Arabs, the Emperor and the British.

It had been after I had found the gold yen in the market at Addis that London had really hardened up. Somebody was supplying naphtha to the Japanese motherships in the Red Sea which serviced their submarines in the Indian Ocean. I had traced the gold yen back to one of Jonnet's outfits in Addis. And there was nobody else who even had sufficient fuel to interest the Japanese navy. But the warning from London had been clear. 'Don't pull in Jonnet until you've got evidence that would stand up in court.' It would have taken me at least another two months to get that, and even then I should have needed a lot of luck. I could have got him on arms-smuggling, but we had wanted him on bigger stuff than that.

* * *

8

Kathi Kathikis was beautiful, and once she must have been just pretty. But in those days, when I was twenty-two, ladies in their mid-thirties had seemed fairly ancient to me. She'd been one of my main informers on the Palace. She advised the Emperor on business, she said. And her enigmatic smile could be interpreted how I liked. I could never imagine the old boy stripped for action but I could well understand the need for an alternative to the Empress. And in terms of business or scandal there wasn't much that went on in Addis that Kathi didn't know about.

I'd learned a lot about Jonnet's deals with the Palace from her. She admired his ruthlessness and his business skill but she didn't like him as a man. If she had liked him she wouldn't have talked. Jonnet's son was married to a ravishing Italian girl. She was only eighteen. The son had seen her in the civilian prison camp in Mogadishu and had married her two months later. Jonnet senior had had her too, whenever he fancied and whenever his son was away. Even night-club owners felt that that was going a bit too far.

A lot of people had waited years to see Jonnet get his comeuppance but it had never happened. I sensed that in those days a lot of people saw me as the one who might bring it off, and I'd built up a solid network of informants around him. But if I put him inside while short of evidence, then lots of heads would roll. And mine would be at the very bottom of the pile.

There hadn't been much of a crowd that night. A few rich Arabs and Greeks, and a sprinkling of people from the embassy and our military mission. The word had obviously gone out and they never quite noticed me.

I was dancing with Kathi when he came in. He was about thirty but bald at the front. I saw him standing there looking for me. The band was playing 'J'attendrai' and Kathi was singing it in Greek and it sounded very sad.

By two o'clock that morning I'd handed over. His name was Peers, Logan Peers, and he'd been recruited into MI6 from one of those fancy regiments that wear chain-mail on

9

their shoulders on Mess nights. He had listened attentively as I went over the saga of Jonnet. Command had said burn all records so it was all word-of-mouth stuff. He'd got those small eyes that seem to take everything in without moving about much, and I had the feeling that he would have Jonnet in the bag before too long.

By the time I was ready to leave, Kathi had heard from someone that I'd had the chop. As I went to leave she took my hand and led me into her office. She kissed me, not quite like a mother, and put something into my hand. *'Seulement à donner de la bonne chance,'* she had said. It was a beautiful silver coin. A Maria-Theresa dollar. I slipped it in my pocket. And I always have been lucky. Nearly always, anyway.

The war had been over for five years before I saw Peers again. As so often happens when you haven't seen someone for years I saw him twice in the same week. The first time was at the Travellers' where I was somebody else's guest. He had been sitting on his own at the far end of the dining-room. When our eyes met he was about to sign his bill. Our eyes meshed for a second and then he had turned away as if he didn't recognize me. The second time was in Wheeler's. He was with a woman and I was shown to the next table. There was no possibility of avoiding each other and we shook hands with the excessive affability that always happens in those circumstances.

He introduced me to his companion. She was his wife, and they were going on to the theatre. I sat with them for a drink and I noticed the woman looking at me with unusual interest. After a few moments' guarded talk about the old times she had interrupted me, and with a slight French accent she said, 'I know now who you are. You're Johnny Grant. My father's told me all about you.' And she was smiling. An odd sort of smile. Knowing and amused.

'Sounds interesting. Who's your father?'

Peers looked embarrassed and he lifted his glass.

'That's all a long time ago, Sabine. Best forgotten. Let's drink to Johnny now.'

She opened her mouth to speak, thought better of it, and still half smiling, raised her glass.

'*A la vôtre,* Johnny.'

Back at the flat at Ebury Street I poured out the drinks and waited for Joe Shapiro. After I was thrown out of Addis London had sent me down to the Ogaden, that wild territory on the borders of Somalia and Ethiopia. There was, by then, a lurking suspicion that His Imperial Highness was playing footsie with Jonnet in his games with the Japanese and shrewd minds in London thought that maybe a small but cheerful war on his southern borders would help concentrate His Highness's mind in other directions. Six months later I had been posted to Italy, and after that I worked with Joe Shapiro in Germany.

When I left, in 1947, Joe had stayed on in the racket, and now he was something in the section that specialized in counter-punching the Russians. It was Joe who had got me my promotion to major and we'd kept up a desultory but genuine friendship ever since.

I sometimes did a bit of photographic work at the studio for the old firm, and the business came through Joe. It didn't pay like the commercial stuff but it meant that when I needed them I got visas and passports in hours not weeks. It looks glamorous enough to be carting off half a dozen pretty models to some exotic spot but the admin can drive you mad. And that's when Joe's help was invaluable.

We had talked and drunk for about an hour before I mentioned meeting Peers and his wife. Joe had never heard of Peers but he humoured me and said he'd check on her father for me.

It was a week later when Joe phoned me at the studio. I'd almost forgotten about Peers.

'Peers's wife, Johnny. She was a Sabine Jonnet before she married. Her old man's name was Marcel Jonnet, a

11

merchant in the Middle East somewhere. Your old stamping ground, so that's probably why she'd heard of you. And Peers is still in SIS. I ought to have remembered his name. I've seen it on summaries from time to time.'

'What does he do, Joe?'

'According to the book he's still on the African desk. But what it says in the book ain't always true of course.'

No wonder they'd never got Jonnet. Whether he contrived it or whether it just happened, he must have been laughing. To have the MI6 man who's been briefed to get you, marry your daughter, was a better insurance policy than the Prudential could offer you. I told Joe the story but he didn't seem all that interested. And there I was wrong, but it was twenty-five years before I found that out.

Joe and I had gone to a concert at the Festival Hall together. It was a Menuhin night and of course the applause had been rapturous. It wasn't just the Elgar, it was the awareness of all those years ago when the infant prodigy had first played the concerto for the grand old man. He'd listened at rehearsal to half the first movement and then he had held up his hand. And instead of carrying on with the rehearsal he'd taken the boy to the races. And now that boy, a mature man, stood beaming, despite himself, at the genuine love and enthusiasm that came from his audience. Then he had held up his hand, and in the silence, had played, unaccompanied, the little Beethoven Romance. The feminine one. You knew you were at one of those nights that people would talk about in fifty years' time.

We went down to the Festival Hall self-service place for a cup of coffee and a bun. There was snow coming down outside, big gentle flakes that had already laid down a couple of inches of whiteness on the grass mound and the benches outside.

I offered Joe a cigarette but he'd shaken his head and shuffled his empty coffee cup to one side.

12

'How's business, Johnny? You busy?'

'Fair to medium. I've been taking it easy for a couple of weeks.'

One of his stubby fingers was pushing crumbs into a little heap on the red Formica tabletop, and then he looked up.

'We'd like to use you for a couple of weeks.'

'More of those ugly Russian faces for your portrait gallery?'

He shook his head. 'No. It's overseas, not here.'

'Where overseas, Joe?'

'Addis Ababa.'

I laughed. 'What do you want? The Imperial family at home in Addis jail?'

He wasn't amused, and he showed it.

'You remember that fellow you met – Logan Peers and his wife?'

'Sure.'

'And her old man, Jonnet?'

'I remember him all right.'

'Well, we think Jonnet's up to his old tricks again, and we'd like you to give him the once over for us.'

'They'd clobber me as soon as I got there. Don't forget that I was thrown out.'

He leaned back and looked at me, shaking his head.

'You're a photograper now, Johnny. At the top of the heap. With a reputation. If you took on an assignment out there they'd welcome you with open arms. Their tourist trade needs all the help it can get right now.'

I had visions of fashion shots outside the Gates of Harar and against the Ghebbi walls. They could be good. And they'd certainly be original. Joe interrupted my thoughts.

'How much d'you normally get for that sort of assignment?'

'Standard charges, Joe. Three hundred a day plus model fees plus travel and subsistence for all concerned. It's quite a heap of dough. Depends on the client. If it's

13

the kind of assignment that brings more business I sometimes do a package deal.'

He shrugged. 'That'd be OK by us. Say fourteen days at
your discretion.'

'When have you got in mind?'

'Soonest.'

'I'd need time to make some deal with a fashion house.
That could save you up to half the cash and I'd need the
latest stuff or somebody would soon rumble that it was
phoney.'

'We can help you there maybe. But that part's only the
cover, remember.'

'What's Jonnet been doing to deserve all this?'

'You've read about the military revolt in Ethiopia, the
executions and all that, have you?'

'I read the newspaper reports and saw the stuff on the
TV news programmes. Nothing more than that.'

'And what was your impression?'

'Surprise that the media took it all so seriously. There's
always been outbreaks of fighting there. One warlord
fighting another. It's always been feudal. But they repor-
ted it all so seriously. Referring to men as Ministers of this
and that, who were just the usual crafty bastards you get
in that sort of country.'

'You didn't read anything more into it?'

'No.'

'How would you rate the Ethiopians against the other
African States?'

'Oh, top of the league without a doubt. Smart as they
come.'

Joe smiled. 'That's what our people think, even if it's
put more formally. We think these new boys have got big
ideas.'

'Like what?'

'Like taking over the whole of East Africa. Kenya,
Somalia, Tanzania, Uganda – the lot.'

Even in the few seconds while Joe was saying it out loud
it seemed terribly possible. They could do it now that the

14

Emperor was out of the way. But they'd need a lot of outside help. As I looked at Joe it was as if he were reading my thoughts.

'The Chinese have been building up their influence all over East Africa. The Russians would spend a lot of time and money to teach their old friends in Peking a lesson. The Soviets have got a bigger mission in Addis now than all the European countries combined. And we think that Jonnet is their man.'

'Doing what?'

'Well, that's the main reason for asking you to make this trip. We don't know all that much. He's certainly very thick with the revolutionaries. Fed them a lot of anti-Emperor dope, and he almost lives with them since the coup. There are meetings almost every day at his villa, and there's money pouring in like water. The Americans have been getting strong hints that it's time they packed their bags.'

'Who's the head of the mission for the Russians?'

'Nominally a guy named Vonikov. You can read our files on all of them. But the man who matters in the mission is Panov. Vasili Panov, a KGB colonel. Let's get back to my office and I'll show you what we've got.'

The aluminium case was under the seat. I'd decided that the Hasselblads and two extra lenses would cover what I needed. Two Weston meters, twenty packs of professional Agfachrome-S and thirty packs of FP4. The small compartments were filled with filters and the usual gubbins. And there was two thousand pounds' worth of sovereigns inside the foam-padded velvet lining of the lid. Ethiopians never trusted paper money and even way back in 1942 they wouldn't take lire or East African shillings, so once a month a plane flew up to Addis with three half-hundred-weight bags of English pennies for me. I paid informants by the scoopful and everyone was happy.

The Linhof tripod was tucked up on the rack with the flash unit. I hadn't worked out any shots in advance

15

because I guessed Addis would have changed. I was booked into the Addis Hilton and that was change enough. In the old days it was the tatty Hotel Imperiale or nothing. The first Christmas after the liberation the hotel had gone very festive, and the balloons, which were originally made for more prophylactic purposes, had made a proud display. I'd given them an honourable mention in my report to London. Our embassy in Addis got copies of certain parts of my reports and I remember the Minister's comment on my balloon report. 'More suitable for the *Daily Express*.' I still take it as a compliment.

The two models were coming over the next day so that I could have a clear day to look around. I was hoping I should find one local lovely, untouched by human hand and never been photographed before, because Somali girls, Abyssinian girls and the Seychelloise are the handsomest girls in the world. Well, they were in 1942.

I'd read all the SIS files on Jonnet, the Russians, the revolutionary *derg* and the influential riff-raff of Addis. I felt like Soames Forsyte would have felt looking at the last episode of the series. Old friends and old enemies had gone from one racket to another. Bribing and conniving their way to corner some market or other. It made a wonderful read, because people who had spent half their lives on the straight and narrow went to pot in Addis in weeks. And from the reports they all seemed to live happily ever after. The class of '42 were mostly winners.

In the old days Addis had been considered an ideal training ground for counterintelligence staff. Cosmopolitan, corrupt, a centre for arms running, dope-smuggling, vice and bribery. And on top of it all the Italians had put a patina of civilization. Had we given them another fifty years Abyssinia would have been a veritable paradise. They had poured in millions, pounds not lire, and they had shown what could be done. It was a sad place after we clobbered them. They'd done a good job all over their bits of Africa. And never fall for the line that they were poor soldiers. They are romantics. One Italian soldier all on his own, with the limelight on him, and maybe with a flag, was as brave as they come. It was just that in groups they couldn't cut a dash. That old Italian vice of *fa' figura* has a lot to answer for.

It was late that night when we landed and the smell in the Customs section was the old familiar smell. Acrid, African, and vaguely exciting. The taxis used to be tiny Fiat Topolinos and they had needed a push to get to the top of the hill, but the taxi that took me to the Hilton was a brand-new Merc, with matching charges. Times had obviously changed.

2

Whether it was jet lag or just the effects of a long journey, it was midday before I awoke. There was a tray of cold toast and barely warm coffee on the table by the bed, and an envelope propped against the milk jug. I knifed it open. It was on Hilton notepaper and said:

Johnny,
Saw your name in the register. Is it holiday or an assignment? I'm room 178. Call me.

Sandy Martin

Sandy was one of those pouchy-eyed foreign correspondents who sit it out wherever there is trouble. They drink too much, smoke too much and generally rate a *Times* obituary when they die aged fifty-two. In any trouble-spot, they can sort out more of the basic facts and quite a lot of the trimmings in two days than most people could find out in a year. Those red-veined cheeks under the tan were part of their cost of living and the eyes that were always half closed against cigarette smoke saw through the official camouflage as if it wasn't there. I should need to tread very carefully with friend Martin.

I rang for room service and the waiter was a young Galla. Fuzzy hair, flat nose and a snow-white *shamma* – the loose Somali robe – that was draped stylishly to reveal his white jodhpurs and bare brown feet. He bowed slightly.

'*Tanasterling getuch.*' And the old-fashioned, respectful greeting took me back thirty years.

* * *

18

When I'd finished bathing, the coffee and rolls had been laid out on the white table on the balcony, and I sat looking out over the town.

There were large white buildings that hadn't been there in my day, with notices and signs in Amharic script, and English or French. But down the slope of the hill I could see the tin-roofed shacks that were the real Addis. And the blue-gums, slender, tall and shimmering in the midday heat. The eucalyptus trees that Menelik had had planted so long ago, and that had finally taken over the whole of the city. They'd called the city Addis Ababa – the New Flower, and despite its squalor they were right. With the possible exception of Harar there is no other city in the world like Addis. There was a vital spark in the people, hard to describe, because it was not connected with energy, and definitely not with progress. It was something to do with eternal things, biblical things. Somebody once said that we all know what went on at Sodom, but what went on at Gomorrah? The people of Addis would know. There was no vice, no lust, that couldn't be slaked in Addis but it didn't spoil the lush tropical beauty of the New Flower. For me, Addis, like Samarkand, would always be romantic, but it could well be nothing more than the effect of a city eight thousand feet above sea level.

I hired a car and driver for the rest of the day and checked over half a dozen shooting sites. The sessions would have to be early morning or early evening because the midday light was too fierce for both film and girls.

I had been able to do a deal with Nelbarden International, the swimwear people. With Joe Shapiro's money behind me I'd been able to put together a deal that was impossible for any other good studio to beat, and the studio's reputation did the rest.

I spent two hours making notes and sketches. It wasn't going to be difficult.

* * *

19

It was a little after eight when I went down to dinner. I just wanted a snack and I strolled across to the Kaffa House. I was well into the asparagus when they paged me. I took the call in one of the phone cabins in the foyer. It was Daphne calling from Cadogan Square. The line was loaded with static, and so was Daphne.

'That you, Johnny?'

'It's me all right. You get my note?'

'Of course I got the damn thing. It was waiting for me when I got back from the country. Why the hell are you in Africa?'

'Like I said – working.'

'Who for?'

'Nelbarden, the swimsuit people. Like I said in my note.'

'Like what?'

'Like I said in my note,' I shouted.

'Who are the girls?'

'New ones. Chosen by the client. Can't remember their names.'

'Liar. I know you.'

'Anything special?'

'What? I can't hear you.'

'You call for any special reason?'

'Freddie Lane proposed to me at the weekend.'

'Congratulations.'

'What? This line's outrageous.'

'I said congratulations. When's the happy day?'

'You really are a bastard, Johnny. I told him I'd think about it.'

'Well, his old man's only a life peer after all.'

'That's true.' There was a pause until the penny dropped. 'Are you taking the mickey?'

'Never, darling. How about I call you in a couple of days.'

'When'll you be back?'

'Another ten days or so. Not certain yet.'

She did a little more interrogation and checking, and that was that.

Daphne Partridge was coming up to thirty and she'd added me to her collection a couple of years ago. Every society girl wanted her own Earl of Lichfield and the younger ones were all spoken for. She was very pretty with blond bouffant hair, good figure and long showgirl's legs, but behind the big blue eyes there was something odd. Something wrong. Down in the country at her parents' place the busy, rather domineering girl became a domestic drudge. Scrubbing floors that were clean, endlessly washing up. Her father was a retired brigadier and they weren't hard up. I always thought her mother was what was wrong. Plump, alert, and watchful she sat in 'her' armchair sewing, knitting and doing fancy embroidery. But behind all this feminine activity she ran a pretty tight ship. On my first few visits I'd been tolerated by Moma but as time went on a perceptible chill set in. Apparently unnoticed by anyone else. I was found little jobs to do and sometimes when I ignored the day's orders there was talk of mother's 'heart'. She wasn't the first woman to play the heart bit to get her own way but Daphne was shrewd enough and old enough to have rumbled the ploy. But if she had, she still went along playing the little girl role. As an account director at one of the big American-owned advertising agencies in London the little girl bit looked vaguely sick if you had seen both characters at work. But I guess we all have our funny ways, and blonde Daphne was pretty, intelligent, and, cutting out the rationalizing, naked she was really something. Moma wouldn't have liked what she did. We had never actually discussed marriage but we'd tramped round the edges of the subject with neither party seeming to come to any conclusions. She liked the social game and I didn't, but apart from that there were no hindrances. Except, of course, Moma's heart and a small awareness on my part that, despite the serious Sundays' women's pages

21

and *Playboy*, love in marriage might last longer than lust. Both parties had wandered from time to time from the straight and narrow but always the sexual jigsaw had drawn us back.

Sandy Martin was sitting at my table when I got back.

'I heard you paged, Johnny, so I tracked you down.'

'Fine. What're you drinking?'

He smiled. 'Always faithful, my boy. Whisky, no water, no ice.'

I told them to bring a bottle of Bell's and we went up to my room.

Sandy stretched himself out on my bed, the pillow doubled up behind his head, and the bottle and a tumbler on the bedside table.

'Daffers not with you, Johnny?'

'No, not this time. That was her phoning from London when they paged me.'

'You on an assignment?'

'Yep. Swimwear. The models arrive tomorrow.'

'How long are you staying?'

'A week's shooting and I may stay for another week to have a break. And you?'

'Just waiting for it all to happen as usual.'

'I thought the revolution was all over bar a bit of shouting.'

The half-closed eyes looked at me through the smoke and the twisted smile was there for a moment or so before he spoke.

'You were in Addis during the war weren't you?'

'Just a few months.'

He turned to stub out a cigarette. He seemed very intent on watching the operation as he spoke again without turning his head.

'You got a work permit?'

He looked up, smiling as he waited for my answer.

'No. But I can get one if I need one.'

'You need one, matey. But I doubt if you'll get one.'

22

'Why the hell not?'

'You see the local paper today?'

'No.'

He grinned, that knowing journalist's grin.

'Just a couple of small paras and a picture.'

'Saying what?'

'Saying that they threw you out in 1942 and that you were close to the Emperor.'

'I was, but it was he who threw me out, for God's sake.'

'These boys are politicians. They're just firing a couple of shots over your head.'

'Why?'

He laughed softly. 'Don't play it dumb, Johnny. You were MI6 and they rumbled you. They just wonder if you're up to your old games again. So do I.'

'Your London office will tell you that I do a ten-hour day at the studio. There's no time for anything else.'

He shrugged, still smiling. 'They told me just that.'

'So?'

'Like the guys at the Ministry here, I still wonder.'

'Which Ministry?'

'The Interior. They control the security boys and the Imperial Guard.'

'They must be more imaginative than they used to be if they cobbled this together as a story.'

He shook his head.

'No, they're not any brighter. They got a hint. Somebody jogged their elbows.'

'Who?'

He swung his legs off the bed on to the floor and picked up his jacket. As he stood up he bent over and screwed the cap back on the bottle.

'Let's keep in touch, Johnny.'

He let himself out.

They started at the airport the next morning. The girls' visas weren't acceptable. The little man in khaki had obviously had his orders so I phoned the embassy. The consul himself would come out, which was a change from the old days. I sat and waited, and the girls were kept in the outer office.

The embassy Jag had been waved through to the terminal building itself and the consul was out to impress. He waited for the driver to open his door and when he got out he unwound to over six feet. He nodded to me and then walked into Immigration. He was in there for about five minutes and then he got back into the Jag without even a glance in my direction. The girls came through a couple of minutes later. I got the message. The embassy had obviously had orders to help but they weren't going to fraternize. They had long memories too.

Back at the hotel I gave the girls the afternoon to rest, and in the evening I showed them half a dozen of the shooting spots I'd picked out. Then we had dinner together and they went back to their room early. We were shooting at seven the next morning.

3

By 6 A.M. I had checked over all the equipment and packed it into one aluminium case. Two Hasselblad bodies, a standard lens and a 250-mm Sonnar, meters, flash, filters and two lens hoods. I stuffed the film packs in my bush-jacket pockets, and was ready for the fray.

The girls were on time and the driver was sitting on the steps in front of the hotel. We headed for the lake at Bishoftu.

When the Italians surrendered they had been put in POW camps or civilian camps. The civilians had been repatriated to Italy over the next twelve months, and most of the soldiers had been sent down to camps in Kenya. But the Emperor and a few other worthies had kept a handful of Italians out of the network. They repaired radios and cars, and some even practised law or ran restaurants. One of them was Emilio Biffi, a lively, grasping Sicilian. He had run the hotel at Bishoftu, and the Italian colony assembled there in the old days, on Sundays and holidays. Whatever you wanted, Biffi could get it. Spare parts for Fiats and Lancias, those precious red valves for radios, tyres, naphtha and petrol, booze and girls. There was a time when my own petrol came from Biffi. The military mission had refused to supply me. It wasn't just for the sake of my blue eyes, for the Italians had seen through my cover a bit quicker than the Ethiopians. Apart from that, I'd been able to get Biffi's wife's name removed from the repatriation list so that she could stay on with him. When I'd been doing my recce for suitable photography sites I'd gone out to the

25

hotel. Biffi had been away in Asmara but was due back the next day. I'd left a message.

The welcome was effusively, delightfully, Sicilian even at eight in the morning, and the signora had the coffee and rolls already laid out for us. There were kisses all round, and ten minutes or so spent talking about the good old days.

The hotel was covered with bougainvillaea and there were jacaranda trees lining the path down to the lake. The girls and I went through the basket of swimsuits and sorted out the main items. When they came out half naked there was much comment from Emilio until we set off down to the water.

I had miscalculated the sun's position and that meant lugging the equipment halfway round the lake so that I could get the water and the sun behind the girls. But at the end of the first hour I knew I'd got what I wanted. I spent another half-hour getting some more shots with fill-in flash because there was a breeze off the lake that was doing nice things to the girls' long hair. I was sealing the exposed film in a plastic bag when a small Ethiopian boy came trotting round the shore of the lake scattering the wading flamingos as he came. Ignorant of what his forebears did to bringers of bad news he smiled amiably as he gave me a message from Biffi.

'*C'è uno tenente della polizia per lei.*'

'*Dove?*'

He pointed back up at the restaurant.

'*Laggiu al ristorante con Signor Biffi.*'

'*È solo?*'

'*Non, c'è due askari.*'

It was past twelve when we got back up and the lieutenant and his posse were drinking *tej* at one of the tables. The lieutenant waved me over and I ignored him and walked on into the cool shade of the bar. Not because he was black; I just don't like wavers-over and finger-snappers, military or civilian, black or white. I saw Biffi behind the bar and ordered a whisky. He spoke very softly.

26

'Take care, *signor* Johnny. He's got a warrant.'

'OK. If they turn nasty, phone the British Embassy. Tell them what's happened.'

'Sure I will.'

The lieutenant wasn't a big man and that made it worse.

'I call you, Englishman. Why you not come?'

I turned and looked at him. He was wearing the insignia of the Imperial Guard, and his nostrils flared with anger and there were bubbles of saliva at the edges of his mouth. He had a great big .45 Colt with bone handles, stuffed in a worn leather holster on his belt. His right hand was round the butt already. I spoke slowly and quietly.

'I should like to know who you are, lieutenant.'

'Kalema Worq. Lieutenant Imperial Guard. You are under arrest.'

'What's the offence, lieutenant?'

'Working without a work permit. We go now to Addis Ababa.'

'You have a warrant?'

He took the paper from his tunic pocket. It was in Cyrillic script and I couldn't read it. I handed it back.

'Let me make arrangements for the ladies to be taken back to Addis.'

He shook his head. 'They come also with me.'

Biffi was busy polishing glasses and out of the corner of my eye I saw him slowly put one down on the counter. He had picked up my wavelength quicker than the lieutenant had.

'You have warrants for their arrest?'

The dam burst inside him. His face contorted as he shouted, 'They come like I say.' And he pulled out the heavy revolver. I moved outside his arm, clapped both hands round his wrist and swung up. His arm came up, and as he leaned back I levered him over. When that happens to you you can choose one of three things – your wrist breaks, or your arm comes out of its socket or you go over backwards. I'm not sure that he chose, but he went over backwards, and as his head hit the concrete

27

floor he lay quite still. Just to be sure, I put my foot on the hand that was holding the Colt and it slid away from his fingers as the pressure forced them open.

I heard a rifle-bolt slam, and the two askaris were standing in the doorway pointing their rifles at me. I heard Biffi say something in Amharic and one of the askaris replied. There was a short conversation and then Biffi spoke to me.

'They want me to call the Imperial Guard commander. Don't move. They're very touchy, these boys.'

I played statues while Biffi phoned and then he spoke to the askaris and afterwards to me.

'They say I take the girls back to the hotel but you stay here. They're sending somebody out for you.'

The girls, white-faced and frightened, had gone off with Biffi, and the askaris sat with me at one of the balcony tables. I tried chatting them up in English, French, Italian and Swahili, but either they didn't understand or they weren't in the mood. The lieutenant lay on the floor unmoving but breathing. After almost an hour a jeep turned into the car park and a much medalled officer climbed out and walked over. He had a grizzled crew-cut but except for a few more lines the face was much the same. But he wore a general's trimmings this time, and he didn't bother with a swagger stick as he did in the old days. It was Mulugueta.

He walked over to the door and looked at the lieutenant and then back at me.

'You kill him?'

'No I don't think so, general. He's just not back with us yet.'

He hesitated for a moment then walked inside and bent down beside the lieutenant. He pulled back his eyelids and then stood up. He looked up at me.

'Concussed, general?'

He nodded, walked out again to the balcony and spoke to the askaris. They carried the lieutenant to the jeep and I heard the engine start. Mulugueta took my arm and we walked inside the bar. The signora was there, trying to be diplomatic and helpful. He asked if we could use one of her private rooms.

It was cool and old-fashioned, and the general sat himself down in one of the armchairs. I sat down too and we looked at one another. I offered him one of my cigarettes, he looked at the pack and then took one. His face was one of those war-torn faces that both men and women can find attractive. It spoke of violence witnessed and done, of power, and the cunning that preserves men who are thieves among thieves. He looked as though he still took drugs because his eyes still had that smoky glaze. Probably a *khat* chewer. After a few minutes looking at me he relaxed and leaned back.

'Tell me what happened.'

'Your man said I was under arrest and then insisted that he take the girls as well. I asked him if he had a warrant for them and he pulled his gun on me. So I dealt with him.'

He was silent as his eyes went over my face.

'You have a work permit?'

'No, your embassy in London knew the purpose of my visit and said all facilities would be given. They welcomed the publicity, they said.'

'You have that in writing?'

'Yes.'

He held out his hand.

'It's back at the hotel.'

He nodded and stubbed out his cigarette, still watching my face. 'How long did you intend staying?'

'A week or ten days for work, and a week's holiday.'

'They tell me you really are a photographer now.'

'Not just now, general. For the last fifteen years.'

'Like when you were Military Liaison Officer to the old man?'

There was nothing to say to that so I said it. His tongue was digging around his teeth as he worked it all out.

'I think we give you an official escort while you are in Addis. Saves any problems arising. What you say?'

29

'So long as they don't get in my way.'

He nodded his head slowly and stood up.

'Who put the dirt down, general?'

The bushy grey eyebrows went up and he shrugged too easily. 'We all got old friends, captain. We all got old friends.' He smiled. 'Is always old friends who shit on us.' He sighed. 'I take you back to Addis with me.'

The jeep was in the car-park with a driver. He handed Mulugueta a note and he stood reading it.

'Seems your friend the lieutenant got a fractured skull, Mr Grant. I give you his brother for escort, eh?'

Biffi was waiting for me back at the hotel. I looked in on the girls on our way to my room. The fright had gone, they were excited now, and looking forward to more of the same. I disabused them of that idea, partly as revenge for them calling me 'sir'. At my age you get touchy about that sort of thing from pretty girls.

I turned up the radio before we settled down for a drink and Biffi nodded approvingly.

'The black boys don't know how to use electronic bugs, *signor capitano*, but those bloody Russians do.'

'What you want, Biffi, a chianti or a whisky?'

'Whisky with ice, *signor*.'

I took my turn on the bed and Biffi took one of the armchairs.

'I think maybe we better have a little talk, *amico*. I think you not understand how things have changed.'

'Tell me, Emilio.'

'The new boys are very smart and very greedy. Since the revolution they make plenty talk about helping the peasants and social democracy for everybody. All it means is they want their turn at the loot and power. An' they got it, OK. They send all the troublemakers to the countryside to help the peasants, so that removes the intelligentsia and half the politicians. The only politicians who stay are those who do as they are told. The army runs the country now. Nobody moves, nobody speaks, without

30

the soldiers say so. Somebody tell them you were spy in
'42 and make story you might be spy now.'

'Who told them this fairy story?'

'I not know at all as I tell you, but I heard talk about it
before today.'

'Who are the boys who matter?'

'Ato Kebede and Zenabe Tesfae. Tesfae does the
public talking but Kebede is the boss.'

'What about Mulugueta?'

'He's important. But he doesn't really count. Just a
high-grade servant. Does a lot of their dirty work.'

'Anybody else matter?'

'Your old friend.' Biffi's red face looked knowing and
amused.

'Who's that?'

'Jonnet. Marcel Jonnet. The old man.'

'Why is he important?'

'Jonnet still has businesses in Asmara, Addis, Jibuti,
Mogadishu, Nairobi, Kampala – all over East Africa. He
knows what goes on behind the scenes in those places.'

'And?'

'And these boys got plenty ambitions, *signor* – nobody
can put this country right so they do the same as Musso-
lini. Keep taking over other countries. Keeps the people
happy. You ever thought about what happens in Kenya
when Mboya dies? It'll be the Kikuyu versus the rest. The
rest are getting ready now. Who you fancy when Idi Amin
gets his throat cut? Even the Emperor had ambitions, you
know. We got the HQ of the Organization of African
Unity right here in Addis, *amico*. When all these countries
are demoralized they look for a leader. Whatever tribe he
come from he's no good to the other boys. So. A hero
comes out of the north. An Ethiopian hero.' He paused. 'I
put my money on these boys in Addis. If they can wait.'

'But they can't sort out this country, you said so
yourself.'

Biffi grinned and shrugged. 'So they get some help.'

'Where from?'

Biffi got up slowly out of his chair and stood looking down at me. '*Signor capitano*, I know now you not tell me the truth. I think you come here to spy again.'

'What makes you say that?' But I knew. And cursed my stupidity.

'If you just photographer you make guess where they get help and say so. If you spying you want to hear what other people know or say.'

He shook his head slowly, regretfully. 'They cut you up, *capitano*. These boys are tough, and the people from Moscow who control them are even tougher. I suggest you take photos and go home quietly, otherwise they kill you, and is nothing your government can do to stop them or punish them. They don't care any more about London or Paris or Rome. They all in love with Moscow and power and money.'

After Biffi had gone I lay on the bed smoking, and thinking about what he had said. I was in the bath when Sandy Martin came in. I heard the door open and he called out. He came and sat in the bathroom while I soaked. He was smiling as he tapped his cigarette ash into the washbowl.

'I hear you were up to your old tricks today.'

'You're obviously longing to tell me all about it. What have I done?'

He ignored the question. 'I gave you the gypsy's warning about the bloody permit. Why didn't you take the hint?'

I closed my eyes and turned on the hot water with my foot. 'If it hadn't been that it would have been something else.'

'Sure. But why give 'em a trick? Make the buggers count the cards.'

I opened one eye and looked through the steam at him. 'What's Jonnet doing, Sandy?'

I turned off the hot water to show I wasn't hanging on the answer, but he wasn't kidded for a second. As I looked up at his face he was looking carefully at mine. He was weighing me up.

'There's another old friend of yours in Addis at the moment. Been here a week now.'

I didn't ask. He went on.

'Logan Peers. Ex-Captain Peers, Like you ex-MI6. And, like you, maybe not ex-MI6 but still working for them. His good lady's with him.'

I knew then who'd put the word in.

'Where are they staying?'

'At Jonnet's villa on the airport road.'

'Tell me about Jonnet.'

The place seemed suddenly very still and very silent. Like Sunday afternoons before tea, with the old clock ticking slowly, alongside the aspidistra.

'How much d'you know?'

'I've heard he's playing games.'

'What kind of games?'

'With these boys and the Russians.'

He stood up and threw his butt down the toilet and flushed it. He turned back to me as he sat down again.

'I sent a report back to London a month ago. Asked the editor to pass it to your old lot. I don't think he did. They're not playing games, sonny boy. It's all for real.'

'Tell me, then.'

'There are arms coming into Massawa that the black boys couldn't use in a hundred years.'

'Such as what?'

He shrugged with genuine mystification. 'Johnny, I don't know enough about weapons but I know when people are mounting real security. And that's what they've got at Massawa right now. I went up there to have a sniff around. I didn't get within ten miles of the town or the port. It's been evacuated and the Russians control the whole shooting match. Until the Russians started playing footsie with the Ethiopians, the Eritrean Liberation Movement was completely supported by the Russians, just like Somalia was. Russian advisers, arms – the lot. The ELM sent a patrol to see what they could sneak from their old friends. Just a few machine guns and some ammunition, that's all.

33

The Russians got them. They dropped them behind Asmara. And I mean dropped them. From about three thousand feet. I saw a photo. The bodies looked like non-drip jelly paint. The ELM got the message. And those were the people they were supposed to be supporting.

'And just remember that the Russians have been strongly anti-Ethiopia until a few months ago. They've been giving every support to the Eritreans and the Somalis to knock the crap out of the Ethiopians.

'Jonnet is acting as some sort of liaison between the boys here and the Russians.'

'Any proof of that?'

'Nope. Just one little word that's all. I heard a joke last week when I was having a drink with Mulugueta in the Imperial Guard mess. Somebody referred to Jonnet as Panov's *agafari*. D'you remember the word?'

'I do.'

Agafari is the Amharic word for a governor's go-between. The man you had to square before you got an audience. It was both a word of respect and a pejorative at the same time.

'What about Logan Peers?'

'I don't know anything about him except that he's Jonnet's son-in-law. I'd guess he's here because you're here.'

'Why do you think that?'

'Mulugueta implied it. He didn't hide that it was Peers who had suggested that you might be spying, and that they could put the bite on you about the work permit. I heard that in fact you were in the clear. Except for clobbering one of Mulugueta's lieutenants.'

Sandy Martin lit another cigarette before he stood up. 'There's a lot going on here, Johnny. And I've got a feeling that someone's going to pull a rabbit out of a hat in the next few days.' He nodded his head slowly. 'You'd better watch your step, old lad.'

'I will, Sandy. And you.'

He smiled as he walked out of the bathroom.

4

For two days we had successful photographic sessions morning and afternoon. No escort from the Imperial Guard and no problems. I even chanced my luck and asked for permission to have the girls pose with the lions on the Imperial Palace parade ground. We used the Hilton swimming pool, the *magalla*, the native market-place, and a couple of the other lakes just outside Addis complete with pelicans and flamingos.

I saw the girls off at the airport early on the Wednesday morning and handed over the sealed packages of film to the co-pilot. They were already addressed to the studio for processing.

There was a note in my room to ring the embassy. I was put through to the consul who asked me to go over for lunch. His voice made clear that it wasn't just social.

Major Curtis had been one of the original officers who had come in with Orde Wingate's force from the Sudan. Spoke Amharic and Somali, and didn't overdo the heavy diplomat bit. It seemed that Joe Shapiro wanted a report from me immediately and that I was to use the embassy radio and wait around for instructions. I wrote out my report as briefly as I could, and the signals sergeant encoded it. The only hospitality offered me was a sandwich from the radio operator and I sat around reading old copies of *Country Life* and *Punch* until 3 P.M. The reply was brief. Joe Shapiro would be arriving at the airport the next day. He would contact me in due course, and I was not, repeat not, to contact him myself under any circumstances. We had to meet as strangers if we met.

35

After dinner I walked across the square, past the old Palace and down the long street to the *magalla*. It was here that I had first come on the gold yen that linked Jonnet and the Japanese in 1942.

Down the side-streets the late evening sun could get no foothold, and in the bars the Addis harlots were already assembling. They clustered like exotic birds, pretty, alive, and with figures that could certainly provide the poet's 'pneumatic bliss'. To call them prostitutes wouldn't be fair; they were too young, too beautiful, too innocently available; they were biblical harlots straight out of the Old Testament. Their bodies were as smooth and firm and beautiful as babies' bodies and they could be yours all night for a pound, all week for a colobus monkeyskin handbag. A red cross on a door or a wall meant that rooms could be hired with a girl. A sign which had led to much confusion in the old days on the part of visiting ladies from the British Council. After Montgomery took command in the Middle East morality had reigned supreme, and all army brothels had been closed down in forty-eight hours. And although, officially, Monty's writ didn't run in Ethiopia, morality was top priority for ambitious senior officers. One of the brigadiers' wives in Addis had insisted that in the military hospital the mosquito nets of love's victims should be tied with green ribbon instead of the usual military red.

The market was still busy, and there were stalls selling *tej* and *wot*, checked cloth, coffee and tobacco. In some of the wall-shops there was filigree silver, and yellow Abyssinian gold, in bracelets, bangles and long delicate chains. All the usual small heaps of cereals and pulses and corded piles of skins and hides. Goats were tethered, and game birds strung up on poles, alive, with beady eyes as they hung upside down with their wings half open. At the foot of the hill was the same three-storey building and the same faded sign that said *Etablissements Jonnet et Cie*. The big double door to the yard was open and the bulging sacks of coffee went up, to be lost in the shadows of the roof.

There was a new Citroën with CD plates parked along the frontage.

The Citroën had swept past me as I got to the other end of the square. There was a Somali driving it and Logan Peers and his wife sat in state on the back seat. Neither turned their head in my direction although I was only a couple of feet from the car. But the woman's eyes followed me for a moment as it turned right to go up the hill.

The receptionist at the Hilton handed me my key and a white envelope. It was an invitation to a reception at the embassy that evening. 7.30 for 8.00. I got there at 8.15 and there was already a good crowd. Sandy Martin was talking to a tall Ethiopian. A handsome man with a Clark Gable moustache. Seeing me, Sandy waved me over and introduced me. The handsome man was Ato Kebede, and despite the handsome face, his eyes were probably the cruellest eyes I had ever seen outside a zoo. They were yellow rather than brown and the thrust of his head and neck was the same as a cheetah's when it's looking over a herd of gazelle. He had turned and offered his hand, and he held mine in its firm grip as those eyes looked me over. It was actually difficult to look at his eyes, their intensity seemed to destroy my eyes' focus. His teeth were white and even as he smiled; and when he finally let my hand free, his voice was surprisingly soft.

'The photography. Did it go well?'

'It's not processed yet but it should be really special. I hope to find an Ethiopian girl to model for some other shots.'

'Well done. We should be glad of publicity to help our tourist trade. General Mulugueta tells me that there are no problems now.'

I smiled back. 'I'm glad to hear that. Are there any travel difficulties to Harar and Dire Dawa?'

The smooth eyebrows were raised in surprise.

'None, Mr Grant. Enjoy your trip.'

37

And he turned away as the British ambassador touched his arm to introduce another guest.

The other guest was Joe Shapiro. It seemed that Mr Shapiro was a big-wheel in the travel business, come to look over the possibilities of opening up the country for package tours. The ambassador and Ato Kebede took him off for a private chat. I noticed that Sandy was writing Joe's name on the back of his invitation card.

I went off and chatted with half a dozen rogues from the old days. They were all doing well, and, unusually for rich men, they looked happy with it. They talked cheerfully of past misdeeds. Mostly mine. Biffi had joined the group and was telling some complex joke in Italian that featured the Pope and a lady from New York. Just before the punchline the group was joined by a large man. And despite the almost bald head and the pale face I recognized Jonnet. He was smoking a cigar and carefully not looking at me. When Biffi finished his story Jonnet had laughed and clapped his hands. Then, with an actor's double-take he noticed me.

'*Monsieur Grant, quelle surprise, quelle merveille* . . . they told me you were in Addis. How nice to see you again.'

He held out his hand and I noticed the sickness on his face. It wasn't just the tan that had gone, but the health itself. His face was pale and waxen smooth like an altar candle. The big, thick, five-quid ones.

'Monsieur Jonnet. It's nice to see you again too.'

He nodded as some benevolent headmaster might nod to a promising head-boy.

'And now we are no longer enemies, eh?'

'Were we ever enemies, Monsieur Jonnet?'

He drew on the cigar and rocked very gently from the knees. He looked round appealingly at the silent group, shrugging his shoulders and spreading his arms as he turned away from me. He pointed at Biffi.

'Were we enemies, the captain and I?'

'Every man was an enemy in those days, Monsieur

38

Jonnet. Every man was also a crook in those days. We had to be both to survive.'

Despite Biffi's diplomacy Jonnet couldn't let well alone.

'You say the captain was a crook, Emilio. I can't believe it.'

Biffi tried not to smile and held up a podgy hand, counting my sins finger by finger.

'Black-market petrol he had, this *capitano*. Food for two polo ponies he take from the starving Italians. He pay his informers in English pennies they were so stupid. And he sleep with half the pretty Italian girls in Addis. Oh yes, monsieur. He very bad man.'

The tension dissolved in the laughter at my expense. Jonnet put his hand on my arm and said quietly, 'You come and eat with me before you go back, please?' And he looked as though he meant it.

'Of course.'

Biffi and I left half an hour later. We walked to the top of the hill and the moonlight washed across the back of the huge statue of the Lion of Judah in Adowa Square. The statue was so typical of the whole country. The lion so beautiful with its modern, carved stone mane and head, and its elegant body; but from the podium itself the rectangular cladding stone had fallen away to expose patches of worn cement. Beautiful and tatty at the same time. Like Addis itself. There was the strong perfume of flowers and trees on the night air, and faintly, from a distance, were the strains of Glenn Miller playing 'Take the "A" Train'. Biffi said it came from the night-club across the square down towards the market.

It was still called the Star of Ethiopia but it was a lot grander than it used to be. It was never really a night-club. More a friendly brothel with music. In the old days desperate Europeans from embassies and missions had tried to lift it out of its primitive mud, but in the end they gave up. Third Secretaries' wives had danced lan-guorously with attachés, silk scarves draped carelessly across bare shoulders and arms. But they couldn't really compete with the licentious soldiery, dancing with the pretty Abyssinian girls who took it for granted that the sole purpose of the last waltz was to give their partners an erection.

There used to be oil lamps to assist the fluttering, unreliable electric light from a portable generator; but now there were strip lights and neon, chrome and pink glass. Biffi and I sat at a corner table and surveyed the talent. The new owner walked over to us. I recognized the smiling tanned face but I couldn't remember his name. He was an Armenian and we'd met in the old days but I couldn't remember where. He nodded to Biffi, but the smile and the outstretched hand were for me.

'*Signor capitano*. Haluk Kannassian. You remember the uniform?'

And then I'd placed him. He had been in charge of the tailors' shop at the Addis prison in '42. They had made me a mess uniform, a pair of barathea trousers and a tunic. It had taken me years to live down the trousers. They had been modelled on a photograph from *Picture Post* showing King George VI at Wimbledon. I was the only British officer anywhere in the world with turn-ups to his trousers. I hadn't the heart or the skill to cut the damn things off and they became a touchstone, a test of my moral fibre.

'Mr Kannassian, I remember it well. Will you have a drink with us?'

'You are very kind, *capitano*.'

He waved to one of the girls and we all named our drinks. As we sat there, he and Biffi talked business and bribes, and who was fixing what in the latest shuffle in the regime. When he noticed me looking over the girls he gave a vivid description of their hidden attributes and their current state of health.

We had sat there for nearly an hour when she came in. She was the most beautiful girl I've ever seen. Her skin was the colour of a copper beech in winter and it was as smooth as a stone from a seashore. The big eyes were almost black, and her mixed blood gave the whites a smoky tinge. Her features were Nilotic, with a neat flared nose and a soft wide mouth that was so full that it looked too swollen to be kissed. Her upper lip would never cover the two gleaming front teeth. My hand could have encompassed the slender neck. She was wearing a thin cotton dress. White, with fringes at the skirt and sleeves, and the fringes jiggled as she walked. So did her beautiful breasts. She was tall, and her legs were long, and if she had a flaw it was her feet. They were obviously made for walking. For a few moments she looked around at the dancers and then at the tables. She hesitated for a moment and then, recognizing Kannassian, she walked over to our table. I stood up, and Kannassian introduced us. Her name was Aliki Yassou.

'Have any of them been in, Monsieur?'

'No, Aliki. I heard they were at the Jonnet house.'

She looked at a watch on her thin wrist. 'I'd better wait a few minutes.'

'Of course. What will you drink?'

She smiled. 'I'll be a traitor to the revolution and have a Coke.'

She sat down opposite me and it was like looking into a searchlight. She was almost too perfect. Too beautiful. I tried hard to think of her feet. Biffi was telling her about my photography and the pretty models. She smiled across at me. 'You not bring these pretty girls with you tonight?'

'No, they went back to London this morning.'

'To London. How nice. Tell me about London.'

'It's dirty, and full of people and there's probably snow.'

'That I would like. The snow.'

The soft mouth took the straw and she closed one dark eye as she sucked. With the other she looked at me. I plucked up my courage.

'I'd like to photograph you before I go back.'

The last of the Coke rattled in the straw and she put down the glass. She was half smiling as she looked at me.

'You think I would look nice in a swimsuit, yes?'

41

'I'm sure you would, but I meant a portrait.'

She looked puzzled for a moment and half turned to Kannassian. He smiled and pointed at his face.

'A portrait. A picture of the face.'

She looked back at me and the fine eyebrows were raised.

'I am flattered, Mr Grant. That would be nice to have a real photograph.'

She stood up, looking at her watch. 'And now I must go.'

'Can I give you a lift?'

She looked at me for a few moments. 'Thank you, no. I have a car outside. You can contact me through Monsieur Kannassian.' She nodded to the three of us and Kannassian accompanied her to the door. Biffi was grinning at me.

'Don't you try that one, *amico*.'

'Why not?'

'She's private property.'

'Whose?'

'Mostly the Russian mission. In particular Panov. He's their tough guy. They're all tough but he's as hard as rock.'

'She's very beautiful.'

'Addis is full of beautiful girls, *amico*. I show you some of the best tomorrow night. Now I take you back to the hotel and I go home.'

I had expected some contact from Joe Shapiro back at the hotel, but there was nothing. I couldn't even check if he was registered at the hotel in case it connected us. I had half a mind to go back to the Star of Ethiopia and do a deal with one of the girls. Only the thought that Aliki Yassou might get to know stopped me.

5

I was having lunch the next day when the manager of the Hilton came over to my table. There had been a phone call from Ato Kebede. A car was on its way for me. Could I spare him half an hour of my time? Nobody said, 'Or would you rather have your head chopped off?' There was no need to.

It wasn't just a car, it was a Mercedes 600 and there was a crowd standing round the hotel entrance as I got into the back seat. I noticed Sandy Martin on the fringe. The driver turned carefully in the square and that obviously exhausted his patience. We went down the hill like we were at Monaco and as we turned into the road to the airport the offside tyres were scraping the bodywork. You could hear the contact, and smell the burning rubber. The driver looked delighted, and only four of the crowd we just missed actually spat as far as the car. Not that the others didn't try.

We swept into a gravelled drive and skidded to a stop in front of the steps of a white villa. I thought it must be Jonnet's place but I was wrong. There were Ethiopian soldiers mounting guard. In the true style of revolution-aries they were lounging against the walls in tatty uniforms, smoking cigars.

As I was shown into the big room I saw Ato Kebede and Joe Shapiro, talking like old mates. Kebede waved to me to join them, and I ignored my scruples and sat down.

'Mr Grant, I have a favour to ask you. Mr Shapiro here is looking into the tourism possibilities for us. He wants good photographs to show to his people. Would you do them for him while you are here?'

43

'I'm on holiday now, Mr Kebede, I'm not too keen on more work. Surely there must be pictures already on file with the news- and picture-agencies.'

Joe Shapiro nodded amiably. 'Sure there are, Mr Grant. I've seen some of them in London. But they're run-of-the-mill. Record shots. We want high-class stuff. Something that gives the feel of the country. The romance, the atmosphere. And anyway we want to commission them, we want the sole rights. We should pay accordingly, of course.'

I leaned back as if I were giving it due consideration. 'Would they be used in advertising, brochures and so on?'

'We should want the unencumbered rights. No restrictions.'

'That's pretty expensive, Mr Shapiro. Could I offer them myself on an agency basis?'

Joe shook his head. "Fraid not, Mr Grant. They would have to be for our sole use.'

'What are you offering?'

'How about you suggest a fee?'

'How many locations?'

'Addis, Harar, Dire Dawa, Asmara, maybe the port up there. What's it called . . . Massawa.'

'That's going to take two or three weeks.'

Ato Kebede held up a hand. 'I'm afraid Massawa is out for security reasons.'

I shrugged. 'OK, that could save us a couple of days. Say two thousand and all travel and subsistence.'

Joe slowly shook his head, looking vaguely like Topol in matchmaking mood as he did so.

'Fifteen hundred I could go to. Not more.'

'Split the difference, seventeen-fifty?'

Joe stood up, walked around the chair and stood looking out of the window. Finally he turned, and he didn't look pleased.

'Sixteen hundred and that's final.'

I hesitated for only a couple of seconds. Joe didn't like to be teased even if it was in a good cause.

'OK, Mr Shapiro. It's a deal. When do you want me to start?'

'Tomorrow morning. OK?'

'Sure.'

I was shown out and the two great men continued their chat.

I phoned through to London to order more film and a neutral density filter. They said they'd get them out on the next plane and cable the ETA.

All morning I'd been thinking about Aliki Yassou, wanting to phone Kannassian, but not wanting to stick my neck out. I asked the operator to get me the number. Kannassian himself was on the line.

'Good afternoon, Mr Grant. What can I do for you?'

I could tell from his voice that he knew what I was going to ask.

'I want to contact Miss Yassou about her photograph.'

'Ah yes. She did telephone me. She said to tell you if you called that she not going to be available. She apologize very much.'

'I see.'

'How about you come along to the Star tonight. I show you two special girls. They not here for general dancing. They both sixteen, got new doctor's certificate. Very pretty girls, very well-developed, they do anything you want. Maybe you take one on your safari.'

'What safari?'

'They say you go with the English who come about tourists. Take pictures for him.'

'I'll see you tonight, Mr Kannassian.'

'Be fine.'

I felt very flat. I'd only seen the girl for twenty minutes, if that, and I felt like a disappointed lover. Flat, and almost sad. I'd looked forward to seeing her again. In the middle of all this Joe Shapiro rang.

'Ah, Mr Grant. Shapiro here. I've moved into the

45

Hilton. I gather you're here too. We'd better get our heads together. How are you fixed?'

'I'm free when you are.'

'How about you come down. I've got a suite, the number's . . . just a minute . . . yes, it's seventy-two.'

Five minutes later, as he opened the door, Joe stood back with his finger to his lips, and when I went in he talked with his hearty voice on.

'Let's hire a car and you show me the town, eh?'

We sat on a bank at the side of the road about six miles out of Addis, and in front of us the hill sloped gradually away, down to a cluster of *tukals* where a handful of skinny cattle were grazing. The Thermos of coffee was leaning on a tuft of celandine between us. Joe emptied his cup and turned it upside down as he shook out the last drops.

'This report you sent back about the military stuff at Massawa. You found out any more?'

'No, I haven't even tried. Sandy Martin is already suspicious that I'm here to spy. So is practically everyone else. I didn't want to blow it all.'

'I can fix for Martin to be recalled. That would get *him* out of the way.'

'He said he'd sent a report to his editor to pass on to your people.'

'Yeah. It was passed on but it must have got lost in the wash. And it was uncorroborated by any other source. But now the Americans have had the pressure put on them by these chaps to get the hell out, so they're cooperating with us as the sole survivors. They've shown us some satellite photographs covering Massawa. There's a hell of a lot of activity, but all the hardware's under cover. There's some pictures covering the unloading of the ships, but most of it's crated or tarpaulined. Anyway, whatever it is, the Russians are making a five-course meal out of it, and it's now got top priority from us until we find out what it is and what it's all in aid of. You and I need to

46

hot foot it up to Asmara as soon as we can. I looked in your "P" file and I see you had some months there during the war.'

'Only a couple of months, Joe, and I was only rounding up the Italian stay-behind people.'

'You got any contacts there?'

'I had a few in the old days. God knows if they're still there.'

'We'd best see what we can scrape up with these Eritrean boys or some of the Somalis. They need arms and money. If they'll play ball maybe we can help them.'

'Would our people go that far?'

Joe snorted. 'They'll go as far as it takes, Johnny. With the Russians controlling the Indian Ocean, the Red Sea and a quarter of Africa, they'd be sitting on half the Monopoly board.' He spat into the dust on the road. 'I'm glad you argued the toss about the photography. I think they took it all in.'

'You can never tell with those bastards. They're very touchy at the moment, very suspicious.'

'Aw, let 'em be suspicious. As long as they can't prove anything they'll have to go easy with the rough stuff.'

'Joe, this is Abyssinia. They could knock us off here and now and there'd be no corpses and no inquests. They still cut off thieves' hands if they're found guilty.'

'Do they now?' He nodded approvingly. 'Maybe we need that back home.'

I went out at about ten to Kannassian's place. He took me into his private office and sent for the two girls. One of them was a Somali girl from Mogadishu, and she was certainly special. Kannassian had good taste in girls. She'd grinned when I looked her over and she had hoisted up her sweater to show me her firm young breasts. When we were on our own again Kannassian leaned forward and put his hand on my arm.

'Forget the other one, Aliki, *capitano*. OK, she very pretty, but so are these girls. She not got anything the

47

little Somali girl not got. She just a whore the same as the rest of them. She make more money than the others because she get screwed by the Russians. If you want her all that much I fix it for you. But only if you not hooked on her, eh. I fix you have her for one hour, yes? Then you finish. No big eyes, no poetry, eh?'

But I knew that that wasn't what I wanted. Or at least, it wasn't only that. The young Somali girl grinned at me as I went through the front office and out of the side door.

The phone ringing fetched me up from a mile-deep sleep, and I dropped the receiver before I finally got it to my ear. It was dark and the luminous dial on my watch showed 4 A.M. local time.

'Grant speaking. Who is it?'

There was a moment's silence at the other end, and then as I opened my mouth to bark again, I heard her voice. It was almost a whisper.

'Captain Grant, is that you?'

'Yes.'

'I was ver' sorry to disappoint you but it would not have been safe.'

'I understand, Miss Yassou.'

'I mean not safe for you.'

I managed a croaky laugh. 'I can look after myself, honey, but thanks for the thought.'

'Did you want to see me?'

'Sure I did.'

'Why?'

I groaned. 'You're beautiful, and attractive, and I felt you were different . . . special.'

'Is that all?'

'God, isn't it enough? OK, I liked you. Liked you a lot.'

There was a long silence and then she spoke carefully and slowly. 'I meet you in one hour, yes? At place of Kannassian?'

'Where are you now?'

'At Russian mission villa.'

48

'Will they let you out?'

'The big men have all left for Asmara; only Habashi soldiers here now. They not stop me.'

I didn't hesitate long. 'OK. In one hour. Five o'clock.'

The phone clicked at her end, and at my end I felt suddenly awake. I sang softly while I shaved and I even bothered about my clothes. It was ridiculous, if not disgusting. I hadn't felt like this since I was about seventeen.

Kannassian let me in and he was pale and unshaven. The paleness wasn't only lack of sleep. He was scared. Scared as hell. He almost closed his eyes so that he couldn't see her when he opened the door to his back office. She was sitting on a black leather couch and she was wearing the same white dress. I pulled up an armchair and sat facing her. Despite the great beauty it was a girlish face, and if it hadn't been for the eyes, an innocent face. The big dark eyes knew much more than Bertrand Russell ever knew, and they didn't look surprised or offended when I couldn't help looking at her breasts. I could see the pointed circles of her nipples through the thin clinging dress. And now she was here it all seemed slightly ridiculous. Meeting a whore in secret, in the early hours of the morning. And if I'd known where I could buy red roses in Addis at five o'clock in the morning I'd have had those too. What was there to say?

She was smiling as I looked back at her face.

'And now you've looked at me again what do you say?'

'I say again you're very beautiful.'

She shrugged and the fine black eyebrows went up again. 'And so were Mr Kannassian's new girls but you not had one.'

'He told you?'

'When I ask. When I press him.'

'So?'

'So he says you want to have me. So I come here for you.'

49

'You didn't mind?'

'Of course not. You looked a nice man. Most men want to have me.'

'But you said there was a risk.'

'There is, but mainly for you. Just now I think ver' little risk, and I wanted to speak with you.'

'What about?'

She smiled and patted the place beside her on the couch. 'I think men always speak more calmly after they have had me.'

She looked at me patiently and knowingly.

'What did you want to speak to me about, Aliki?'

She put a slim hand up to the long black hair and lifted it back over her shoulder.

'You knew my mother, didn't you?'

I shook my head. 'No. What made you think that?'

She smiled that knowing smile. 'Because she sometimes spoke about you. Said you were a nice man, but a tough man. Said you were a spy of some kind, an agent. Said you took her for rides in your car, and sometimes sat on her bed and talked . . . and that you never tried to sleep with her. And she said you wrote to her a long time after you left Addis and said that what she had given you one night had brought you luck. It was a Maria-Theresa dollar.'

And as I looked I remembered thinking all those years ago, that Kathi must have been very pretty when she was twenty.

'You're Kathi Kathikis's daughter?'

'My father was a Somali from Mogadishu. He was a merchant. He was one of the first Ministers in an independent Somalia government.'

'And?'

'And they had him killed.'

'Who did?'

'The Russians, the Somalis, what does it matter who did it?'

'Why? What happened?'

'My father said we had struggled to get rid of the

50

Italians, then the British, and we didn't want the Russians. He said it publicly. They tried to shut him up but he would not keep silent. They hurt Mama first but that made him worse. So they finally killed him.'

'What happened to your mother?'

'They put a scar across her face. But she not die from that. She loved my father very deeply and she grieved for him a long, long time. At the end of a year she caught fever – typhoid. She made no effort to live, and she died.'

'When was this?'

'Two years ago. When I was sixteen.'

'What did you do?'

'They confiscated my father's money and his farm. A Russian protected me. He went back to Moscow and now I am the same with other Russians.'

'With Panov?'

She looked surprised. 'You know of Panov?'

'I've heard his name.'

She looked at me as if my face were a map she had to read carefully, and her voice was a whisper. 'You are *still* a spy? Still an agent?'

'I'm a photographer.'

'Like you were once a liaison officer to the Emperor?'

I said nothing. Just looked at the beautiful mouth. It looked as soft and tempting as fresh raspberries in a bowl.

'I could help you, Mr Grant. I know many things of these people.'

'And then they cut *your* face.'

'Men still wanted my mother even after she was cut.'

'Why should you help me?'

She leaned forward and the long slim fingers of one hand touched my knee in emphasis. 'The Russians will tear up half of Africa. Not for our good, but for theirs. Not even for their good really. Only that chaos here keeps the rest of the world in tension. It was their influence that had my father killed. Their influence that finds money here in Addis for revolutions but not for the starving. They are like mad children, they love destruction. You

51

people never really understand. We Africans understand because we are still savages too. But we have no power, no resistance against these people. Ato Kebede thinks the Russians operate for him. They use him, that is all.'

I needed time to think and I reached into my pocket for my wallet and pulled out a little plastic square with a silver coin in it.

'That's what your mother gave me.'

She held it on the golden spread of her hand and looked at it. She looked up at me. 'And when she gave you this I was not even born. Did she love you?'

'I don't think so. In fact I'm sure she didn't. But we were good friends, real friends. And she helped me sometimes. Told me things.'

'And you really never slept with her?'

'No. Never.'

She nodded to herself as if to learn a lesson. The big dark eyes were shiny with tears but none of them fell. She spoke very gently.

'Do you want to have me here or at the hotel?'

I hesitated for only a moment because I cared too much just to do it like that, but she misinterpreted my hesitation. She opened the white linen bag.

'I brought a doctor's certificate of yesterday. Nobody had me since then.'

There was no resentment in her face, no anger, no disappointment. I pushed the hand and the paper away. I knew that whatever I said after that, wouldn't work. It would look like arrogance not concern. So I smiled, and said, 'Would it be safe at the hotel?'

'Maybe not. Let us stay here.'

Her hand curved to her body and as I watched, the white zip folded apart and her lush bronze breasts slid out from the soft material.

They were big and heavy, but because she was so young they stood out from her ribcage firm and thrusting. As I looked she stood up and wriggled the dress over her hips, and my eyes were aware of the full breasts jiggling with her efforts, and the triangular black thatch between her legs. She stood there with her long shapely legs astride, and it was obvious that she knew exactly what men wanted of her and found no embarrassment in pleasing them. When I finally looked up at her face she was smiling. A tolerant, accepting smile. She put her head on one side as she spoke.

'You like me this way?'

I nodded. 'You're very beautiful. You must know that already. You're exciting, and you know that too. There's two things I want to do.'

The big eyes were friendly and patient. 'You tell me, Johnny. I do both things you want.'

'Promise?'

She laughed and nodded. 'Promise. Tell me.'

'I want to make love to you.'

She nodded. 'Of course.'

'And I want to spend the rest of today with you.'

She looked at me without speaking for a long time. Then she spoke very quietly. 'Yes, we do that.'

I watched her as she walked to the door and turned the key.

It was ten o'clock when the hirecar was delivered, and Kannassian had worked his way through from friendly advice to anger, to try to talk me out of it. I was sorry, because he was obviously disturbed, and concerned for my safety. But we went, and he'd put us up a picnic basket and some bottles.

I drove eastwards on the road that followed the railway line to Jibuti and turned northwards just before we got to Adama. We left the metalled road and took a track that wound its way up a series of hills. Right at the top was a heavily wooded plateau and that's where I parked the car.

We sat looking across the hills. In the valley there was a string of three small lakes and the water flashed and sparkled as flocks of wading birds wheeled up from the surface, hung on a small breeze, and then drifted down

53

like falling leaves. There were small white clouds strung out like chiffon scarves against the deep blue sky, and their shadows moved along the valley, fondling the low hills as they went.

At the edges of the hollow promontory where we sat, there were wild fuchsias laced with the big white trumpets of convolvulus. And where the grass gave way to sand there were bushes of rockroses, magenta, pink, deep crimson, and white. There were mallow flowers like hollyhocks, and in the sand itself those brilliant little flowers that look like a sprinkling of tiny iridescent gemstones. They bloomed and died in a day, and lived their short lives on one night's dew. At the edge of the eucalyptus trees behind us there were masses of African daisies, yellow, orange and bronze, with lance-shaped leaves and soft, white, woolly undersides. Even at midday there were wisps of thin mist on the lower slopes of the hills but the sun held the plateau in its firm, hot grip.

The white dress lay over a spread of tall wild parsley and Aliki sat with her arms around her bent legs, her head resting on her knees. And as she smiled at me the long black hair moved gently in the wind. She reached out one slim arm and her hand touched my leg. I could only squint back at her because of the sun.

'Was ver' beautiful that you bring me out here.'

I laughed. 'When I said I wanted to do two things you didn't think of this?'

She shook her head. 'No, I not think this,' she said softly.

'What did you think of?' And I couldn't have found a good reason why I asked that if I'd tried. Not one that I would like. It was stupid beyond belief.

Both long hands spread wide. 'I think you want to have me some special way that excites you,' she said it without embarrassment, like a pianist who could do Fats Waller or Earl Hines on request.

'You must hate men.'

She curled one slim finger to take a long frond of hair

from her face. Then she turned her face and looked far across the valley. After a few moments she turned her head again and looked at me.

'Only now I not like them. Before I neither like nor hate. They just men. They just do what men need to do to a girl. But they never, never, part of me, part of my life. Never.' The big eyes shone with the intensity of her feeling. She looked down, and her fingers plucked fiercely at the tufts of grass. 'But now is different because of you. Is like being caught in a net somehow. You understand me?' She looked up and her anxious eyes searched my face. She was looking for some sign before she went on. I stretched out my hand and touched her knee. Instinctively the long legs opened but I left my hand where it was. She leaned towards me and laid her cheek on my hand.

'When I spoke to Kannassian he said you like me too much and the Russians might hurt you or kill you. He said you much want sex with me so maybe you have to pretend it not just sex. And when you have had excitement two, three times with me then you could go away.' She stopped and awaited an answer although she had asked no questions. The full soft lips moved almost imperceptibly at her thoughts, like a butterfly's wings move as it lies resting on a flowerhead.

'And what do you think, Aliki?'

She shrugged. 'The part in me that is Somali thinks Kannassian is right. The part that is Greek thinks different.'

'How different?'

'I don't know how to explain, Johnny. Remember I am so much African.'

'Try.'

The dark eyes looked at me carefully for a moment and then she said, 'I think you like to be with me not just for sex. As men like being with other men.' And there were all the differences between Africa and Europe in that sentence. The *Guardian* could have done a double-page spread on the African aspects of male chauvinist pigs just from those seven words. She was so young and so beautiful, and I loved her. And it wasn't just because she was young and beautiful. There were dozens of pretty models in the studio every month. And I had been married once, so I knew that when the chips were really down the vital statistics were neither here nor there. But just as I had learned through the years not to be committed, I knew now that I was ready to put my hand in the mincer again. And instinct told me that this was the girl who wouldn't turn the handle and add my scalp to the trophies on her wall. Perhaps if we had been in London I should have waited longer, but I doubt it. And perhaps if I'd known what was going to happen to us I should have been more cautious. But we weren't in London, and I didn't know. I was free to ask and I asked.

'Aliki – will you marry me?'

'You mean until you leave Addis?'

'No. I mean until I die. I mean marry, not live with me.'

Her head came up slowly and the sun outlined the slender neck. It was like a gazelle looking over the tall brown grass, watching for danger. She was silent for a long time. Then, 'You have thought about all the problems?'

'I haven't thought about *all* of them. But I'm aware of them.'

'And?'

'And they don't matter.'

She nodded. 'So I tell you. Yes, I marry you on one condition. You ask me again when it is time for you to leave. If you then want, I go back with you to marry or just be your girl. Or if you think so, I stay here.'

'But the answer is yes?'

'Oh yes.' She smiled, and nodded her head.

As I drove us slowly back to Addis it all seemed slightly unreal. Had I too been swept along with the spell of Addis, where Europe seemed centuries away, almost undiscovered?

56

I had fixed to meet Joe Shapiro at eight o'clock and that would be the first hurdle. I hadn't mentioned Aliki and he would have taken it for granted that my mind was only on the Russians and Massawa.

I imagined the script. Enter from stage left with local lovely. 'Let me introduce Aliki. Her dad was a Somali, her mum was a Greek, and until today she was resident whore for the Russian mission. We're going to be married as soon as possible.' There was a wide variety of reactions one could expect, ranging from icy disbelief to joining in the hearty laughter. Ah well, there were going to be lots of those little scenes when we got back to London. I toyed with the idea of warning him before it dropped on him. But warn him of what? That she's coloured? That she isn't Africa's one and only virgin? Who the hell did they think they were, and who the hell did I think I was? In London, Paris or New York I should have been at the tail-end of a long queue for Aliki Yassou.

I parked the car and we went up to my room. While Aliki bathed I went down to the foyer. I'd seen a little something in one of the big glass showcases. It took several minutes to find the Armenian who sold the clothes, and another five minutes to haggle over the price. And then I was the proud owner of a linen dress. Bright apricot with a white leather belt, and a pair of matching shoes. All Italian and wildly expensive. When she put it on she looked as if she had come straight from the Via Veneto. She was standing showing it off when there was a knock, and the door opened. It was Joe, and he didn't see her at first. He was opening his mouth to speak when he spotted her.

'Oh. I'm sorry. I'll come back, Johnny.'

And he turned back to the door.

'Don't go, Joe. I want to introduce you. This is Joe Shapiro, Aliki. He's in the travel business. Joe – Aliki.'

He held out his big paw. 'Is he taking pictures of you, Aliki?'

Aliki looked amused. 'I think he's going to, Mr Shapiro.' She looked across at me for some guidance. I decided to dodge the issue.

'You like to join us for dinner, Joe?'

He shook his head. 'No, my boy, I won't play gooseberry, but I'd like to have a word with you about our work.'

I turned to Aliki. 'I'll be back in about fifteen minutes. Can you be ready then?'

She laughed and nodded. Joe Shapiro and I plodded down the corridor to the lift and his suite. When we were inside he switched on the radio, turning up the volume to cover our words, poured us whiskies and waved me to a chair.

'I've had instructions from London to get whatever details we can of the Russian stuff at Massawa, and then we get back quickly to London. They'd like suggestions from us as to how to find out what the Russians are up to.'

'What do you want to do?'

'Head for Asmara and Massawa tomorrow. See how it goes and maybe we come back here to Addis and fish around the Russian mission for a day or two.'

It was jumping into the deep-end time.

'I'd better tell you something first, Joe.'

He looked just like Spencer Tracy being the patient father to the lovely wayward daughter. He didn't ask what it was all about, he just waited.

'I'm going to marry Aliki, Joe.'

His tongue slid around inside his lower lip and the eyebrows went up. He was nodding his head without speaking, as if I'd confirmed some theory of his. He raised his glass to the side of his head and scratched at his hairline.

'Now what am I supposed to say to that, my boy? Register shock, dismay, and disbelief? Caution you about the problems, or talk you out of it?' He paused for a moment to sit down. As I opened my mouth to answer he held up a silencing hand.

'You're a big boy now, so it's up to you. Any idea what it's all about?'

'I care about her. Love her.'

'And what about her ladyship back home?'

'Not the same, Joe.'

He shrugged and waved his glass in a sweeping gesture that combined tension and impatience.

'You reckon you can put this girl on ice till we've done this little job?'

''Fraid not, Joe. She's been living at the Russian mission.'

The glass, and his hand, came to a frozen stop. 'For Christ's sake, what the hell are you up to?'

'It's just a coincidence, Joe. She's not going back.'

'And what's she been doing with the Russians?'

I told him just enough for him to have the basic background, and he leaned back, closed his eyes, and was silent for several minutes. When he turned towards me his voice was very quiet.

'How about her going back and staying there for a couple of weeks and looking out for what we want?'

'Would you have suggested that if she was white?'

He pursed his lips and frowned.

'Maybe not. So what do you propose doing with her while we deal with this operation?'

'She'll have to tag along with us.' I didn't wait for an answer. I stood up and walked over to the door. As I left I said, 'I'll see you tomorrow morning, Joe.'

We had eaten in the Sheba restaurant and back in my room the beds had been turned down. Aliki switched on the radio and tuned the selector to the local station. Radio Ethiopia was identifying itself with its call sign. The thin notes of an Ethiopian flute went over its small theme a couple of times, and then there would be the last news headlines of the day, in Amharic, before the station closed at 11 P.M. I caught the jumbled names of some members of the new revolutionary committee but I couldn't make

59

sense of it. I walked into the bathroom and was cleaning my teeth when I heard Aliki cry out. She was leaning against the wall, her hands spread out each side of her for support.

'Aliki, what is it?'

She shook her head slowly and pointed at the radio. They were playing the last bars of the Ethiopian national anthem. A man said 'goodnight' in Amharic, Arabic and Somali and then there was just the hiss of the carrier wave. I turned off the switch and took one of her hands. It was very cold.

'Tell me, Aliki. Tell me what happened.'

She gave a deep shuddering sigh. 'They've killed Kannassian. It was on the news.'

'Did they say what happened?'

She nodded. 'He was killed resisting arrest.'

'Did they say why he was being arrested?'

'An enemy of the people. A subversive.'

'Why do you think they killed him?'

She walked to one of the chairs and sat down. She looked up at my face as she spoke. 'It was a sign, to me – or perhaps to both of us.'

'You mean Panov was jealous?'

She shook her head. 'No. It's not that *I* was important. There are a hundred other girls they can have. They were just showing that anyone who interferes in their area will be killed. It is like an announcement, a warning. A few weeks ago a man stole a wheel from one of their cars. He was caught before he even got away from the grounds. They just killed him on the spot. Panov killed him.'

'And what did the Ethiopians do?'

'Nothing. They are not their own masters now.'

'Did the Russians contrive the revolution against the Emperor?'

'No. That was the Chinese. But they only helped with planning and money. It was a genuine revolution. The Russians came in when it was over. They picked their men and took over. They offered good prizes.'

'Such as what?'

She looked up at me with a half-smile. 'Johnny, you'd better tell me what you're doing. Maybe I can help you better if I know.'

Then she stood up and her hands were at the straps of the apricot dress. 'Let's talk about these things tomorrow.' The thin material slid down to her feet and she walked over to the bed where I was sitting. She was wiser than I am. She lay face down as I unbuttoned my shirt. She looked like a freshly opened box of Dairy Milk. Smooth, light brown and rounded. There were dimples on her shoulder blades and at the base of her spine. The soles of her long narrow feet were pale pink. She turned towards me as I lay alongside her. As I put my arms round her I pulled back my head to look at her face. It was so beautiful, so perfect, and between her bent arms the soft roundness of her breasts. My hand smoothed her hip and the sweep of her thigh. Part of me felt she was too beautiful to make love to. But it wasn't the part that mattered.

6

I invited Joe up to have breakfast with us the next morning.
I don't know whether it was the sunshine or the orange
juice, but after the dreamlike qualities of the day before we
suddenly seemed more alive, back in the real world. Joe
was relaxed from the start but said very little. Aliki took
charge, and the waiters and chambermaids showed what
they could do. She bothered with Joe, but with me it was
different. As far as Aliki was concerned, everything I said
was not only a pearl of wisdom, but from that moment on,
the law of the land. Joe pretended not to notice until he
ventured an opinion about the colour of the curtains that
conflicted with my own. Aliki's dark eyes opened in horror,
then half closed in anger as she spoke about the effects of
age in inducing colour-blindness. Joe was mildly amused
and bowed to his hostess's dictum. After we had break-
fasted, Aliki left us. She was going shopping in the foyer. I
had told her not to go outside the hotel.

Joe started the ball rolling. He was swirling yet another
orange juice round in the big wide glass. It was taking such
concentration, apparently, that he didn't look up when he
spoke.

'Have you told her?'

'No. But she's guessed. Her mother was Kathi Kathikis.
You must have read about her in my old files. She knew
what I was up to last time I was here. She was one of my
informants. She knew Logan Peers too.'

'Does she know much about the Russians?'

'I haven't questioned her but she undoubtedly knows a
lot.'

Joe put down his glass and wiped his mouth.

'I apologize for suggesting she should go back to them. It was stupid and graceless.'

'Forget it, Joe. Although I love her and she's so beautiful, I too have a tendency to think I'm doing her a favour because she's not white. The more I'm with her the more I know I'm lucky.'

'Will she tell us about them, d'you think?'

'She'll tell me, and maybe she'll tell you.'

Joe grinned, 'Sort of His Master's Voice.'

'I could go back with her to London and you could let someone else take my place.'

He brushed his hand across the grey crew-cut hair. 'I'd already considered that, but you fit the bill too well.'

'In what way?'

'Most of our people have no experience in this sort of place, and those who have I wouldn't trust without a hell of a lot of supervision. And that, I ain't got.'

He stood up, walked to the edge of the balcony and looked across the square. He turned, hands in pockets.

'I think we should take your Aliki on to the team, if you agree. And, of course, if she agrees. It could be more dangerous for us all if she was just hanging around on the edges.'

'I agree, Joe. Let's talk to her and see what she can tell us.'

I was phoning for room service when I heard the shouts and scuffles in the corridor outside the door. Then the door opened and was slammed to. I crashed it open as the man grabbed for Aliki's neck. He caught the top of her dress and as she came towards me, arms outstretched, the thin material tore and came away in his hand. He was a tall man in olive khaki. Camouflage bush shirt and slacks and a leather belt. I pulled Aliki into the room and as I went outside into the corridor I closed the door behind me.

It was nearly six feet across the corridor and my first rush took him back all the way until he hit the wall. Even

63

with his balance gone he lifted a knee for my crotch. I took it on my thigh as his fist crashed against the side of my face. I grabbed blindly for his hair but it was too short to grip on and I brought my fingers stiffly down his face. He swore in some language I didn't know, and a big hand grasped the collar of my shirt. I was whirled round so that I was against the wall, and just before my head hit the wall I saw the glass case of a fire-hose. I ducked, and took a blow on my mouth from a knee or a fist, but I heard him scream as my head crashed under his jaw. I wrenched his hand from my shirt and it came away with a square of khaki in his grip. For a moment both my arms were free, and as his other hand came up I blocked it to one side and I heard my own shout as I went in for a *shuto-barai*. All my body-weight and strength went into that slicing arm, and my mind was in the cutting edge of my hand as it chopped his neck. I heard his clavicle snap, the rattle as his trachea folded, and I felt the foul stomach smells as his breath exploded in my face. He went down backwards and he was out long before his head bounced on the coarse-fibred carpet.

There was a small, silent crowd. Waiters, chamber-maids and a guest or two. Joe was looking judicial and pale at the door. I pushed past him and looked for Aliki. One of those beautiful eyes was swollen and closed. There were scratches on her neck and shoulders and the apricot dress was finished. I took the hand that wasn't holding the damp cloth to her eye.

'What happened, Aliki?'

'One of the Amharas from the Russian mission saw me in the hotel lobby. He must have phoned them. The man who got away was Panov.'

'Where did he get away?'

She looked up with the one beautiful eye. 'The one in the corridor just now.'

'Lady, you just come with me.' And I took her hand.

As we looked down at the unmoving body, I asked her, 'Is that Panov?'

It seemed a long time before she answered. Then she said, 'Did you do that?'

'Yes. But is it Panov?'

'Yes, it's Panov.'

I took her back in the room and she noticed my face. As I picked up the phone she went to the bathroom. I told them to send up the manager and to get me the Imperial Guard on the phone. When I told Mulugueta there was a touch of pleasure in his response.

'You do it with a gun?'

'No.'

'Furniture?'

'No. My hands.'

There was a chuckle. 'Panov won't like that, *capitano*.'

'He wasn't meant to like it. Anyway will you send your men.'

'Better an ambulance from the hospital.'

'To hell with an ambulance. He attacked a lady. My fiancée.'

There was some silence and heavy breathing.

'Who the lady, *capitano*?' And his voice was walking on tiptoes.

'Aliki Yassou, and I want Panov arrested for attacking me.'

'I come down myself.'

Aliki was putting a cold, wet facecloth around various spots on my face and head. And now the excitement was over there was enough pain to keep me quiet.

When the manager came, Mulugueta was with him. The usual manager was away and this was a relief manager. He apologized in about five languages. Aliki's dress would be replaced immediately and he would send for a doctor to attend to me. He left, but Mulugueta stayed. This time he'd got his little stick with him. He had obviously hurried, and there were beads of sweat as he mopped his face and neck.

'The Russians already phoned that I arrest you.'

I opened my mouth in obvious anger and he put up his fat hand.

'We not do that at all. Ato Kebede say that there were witnesses that Panov attacked the girl and this behaviour in public not allowed.'

'But OK in private, eh?'

'They will be very careful now, *capitano*. We are telling Soviet Ambassador officially from Foreign Minister that we do not like this attack on a visitor.'

'And the attack on Miss Yassou?'

The big black face looked as hot and bothered as Louis Armstrong after a session, and he spoke to Aliki in Amharic. She nodded several times. I asked her, 'What did he say, Aliki?'

'Many apologies to me. But say I not go back to them till you leave the country. I told him that I wasn't going back there anyway and that I'll be with you.'

Mulugueta bowed out a few minutes later and there were noises in the corridor for half an hour.

The doctor came in time to spoil our lunch. He was an elderly Italian and had obviously heard the story. As he dabbed and cleaned and plastered he made clear that laying out friend Panov was a popular event so far as the Addis Europeans were concerned, and not too unwelcome to the general populace. When he had gone Joe said, 'What the hell was that last bit you did to him?'

'It's a karate thing called a *shuto-barai*.'

'We'll have to fix you up with a pistol because those boys are going to want to level the score. What do you think, Aliki?'

And by asking her advice Aliki had been brought into the circle. She knew it, and was pleased.

She shrugged. 'Is very much for the Russians a problem. The Ethiopians believe in you as photographer and they want tourism very badly for currency. I think they not like interference from Panov.' She smiled at both of us. 'Is OK to tear up map of Africa but not to beat up foreign photographers in best hotel in Addis.'

'Can you get me a gun, Joe?'

'Sure. What do you want? A Walther, a Luger, or what?'

'I'd like a revolver not a pistol. Will this be from the embassy?'

He nodded, 'Yep. I guess they'll have Colts and Smith & Wessons. I'll fix it.'

Joe had hardly left when there was a knock at the door. The boy thrust forward an envelope. I leaned against the wall and ripped open the stiff white paper. There was a handwritten note inviting me to dinner that evening at Jonnet's place. I phoned Jonnet's office and told his secretary I'd be there with a companion. I phoned down to Joe and told him where I was going but made no comment. Neither did he.

I was about to phone for a taxi that evening when there was a call from reception to say that Monsieur Jonnet's car had arrived for me.

7

We sat in the back of the car holding hands, and it amused Aliki; the holding hands, and the kissing and the talk of love. African ladies weren't accustomed to minor signs of affection. Men held hands, but not men and girls. Women's lib will have a strange, crooked furrow to plough when it gets to darkest Africa.

Jonnet's villa was enormous. It had been built for some Italian worthy in the bad old good old days. The wide sweep of the drive and the magnificent frontage looked like the posters on railway stations advertising building societies, with the owner and his family waving goodbye to the departing guests in their Jag, while the house lights blaze like Blackpool in Wakes week. Bougainvillaea billowed over the roof and hung in great flounces at the eaves. There were no curtains at the big windows and, inside, the rooms were bathed in a soft, warm light. Where the car had stopped there was a large circular pool, with three fountains splashing water on to shoals of big red carp. There were waterlily pads shining under the bright lights, and in small groups there were white ornamental tables and chairs arranged on the patio.

We were shown into a beautiful room, and a tall, handsome Somali in a white shift arranged chairs for us at a bamboo table. A log fire burned in a modern copper fireplace and the light from its flames put a golden glow along Aliki's shoulders and arms.

It was almost five minutes later when Jonnet came in. He was wearing a white linen suit and a scarlet shirt. He was charming to Aliki and friendly to me, but it couldn't

68

disguise his underlying ruthlessness. His eyes never joined in the social chitchat, they watched my face carefully as he listened for clues in everything I said.

We ate round a large oval table and the only immediate light came from the candles in their silver sticks. He had waited until the coffee was poured before he got down to the real stuff. And as he spoke he leaned his heavy body back in his chair.

'I hear you had trouble with the Russians today, Major Grant.' The light brown eyes held mine, and I got the main part of the message. Everybody in Addis still called me *capitano* because that's what I'd been when I was there in '42. Friend Jonnet called me Major to show that he knew that that's what I'd been when I got back to London. And it also implied that he didn't believe that I was now a civilian.

'Only one of the Russians, in fact.'

He smiled a cold smile as he tapped out the long ash of his cigar.

'A very important Russian nevertheless, my friend.'

'Not to me, Jonnet. Not to me.'

The almost invisible eyebrows went up with mock concern as he looked across at Aliki.

'Will you be returning to the Russian mission in due course, *Mam'selle*?'

Aliki slowly shook her head and I was glad that she managed a smile. She didn't speak so I chipped in my little news item.

'Aliki and I are getting married as soon as my photographic trip is finished.'

There was only a second's surprise on his face, but it was several minutes before he spoke. He leaned forward and the candles threw harsh shadows across his face. He was looking at me without any pretence of amiability. He had found his pressure point now and there was no need to go on digging around to find the chink in my armour. His voice was almost a whisper.

'I am not sure, Mr Grant, whether or not you are

69

playing your old games again here. There are many who think you are. So I must warn you . . . with great sincerity. Do not interfere in the affairs of this country. You and I were enemies all those years ago. They were children's games in those days, and even then you did not succeed. But now you would find that there are no prizes. No medals to be won, no promotions, not anything but the most unpleasant consequences.'

As he looked at me I could see that he was breathing heavily, either from the physical effort of his vehemence, or from anger itself.

'Who are you speaking for, Jonnet? This isn't your country, you're an Armenian, and the Ethiopians can speak for themselves.'

His chair scraped noisily on the floor as he stood up.

'We both know what we are talking about, Grant, so I shall say no more. Excuse me for a moment.' And he walked out of the room.

Aliki and I walked out on to the patio and the smell of blossom and flowers was like spice in the air. We sat on the edge of the circular pool and as Aliki trailed her fingers in the water the big red carp moved silently to investigate. She shook the droplets from her long fingers as she looked at me.

'Be very careful, Johnny. This man is more powerful than you think. He has links far beyond the Russians here, right back to Moscow.'

'OK, sweetie. We'll talk about it later.'

Then Jonnet was walking slowly towards us, accompanied by Logan Peers and his wife. The Somali houseboy was carrying a silver tray with bottles and glasses.

After the handshakes Jonnet had held up his hand, and as we waited he reached in his pocket and took out a narrow, rectangular, blue leather case. Looking at everyone in turn he said, 'Major Grant and Mam'selle Yassou are to be married, and if I am lucky this is their first wedding present.' Smiling, he handed the blue case to Aliki. For a moment she hesitated, looking at me, and then she pressed up the catch and lifted the lid. On a base of blue velvet lay a gold cross. Eleven opals were set in the gold, and around the edges was a border of diamonds. The flecks of green and orange in the opals shone out clearly, even in the light of the moon. And as Aliki looked at it, the others watched her face. Finally she looked up at Jonnet.

'It is most beautiful, Mr Jonnet, but . . .'

He held up his hand, smiling and gallant. 'No buts, *Mam'selle*. It is not as beautiful as you but it is much much older.'

'How old is it?'

'Why don't we sit down and I'll tell you.'

When we were all seated and drinks had been poured, he started.

'In the sixteenth century Gondar was the capital of Ethiopia, and in the seventeenth century the small kingdom was ruled by a king. King Fasilidas. He kept his kingdom isolated from the rest of the world, and he built the big castle that is still there. The one with all the turrets. The engineers whom he employed for the operation were Portuguese. One of them had a very beautiful young wife. The king fell in love with her, and the gold cross was made on the orders of the king as a present for her. Two days later she was found at the foot of one of the cliffs. She was dead, and the cross was near her body. Nobody knows what happened to the cross after that until 1890. It was sold in that year by a man who lived in Harar. He was a Frenchman. A poet. His name was Rimbaud. He sold the cross to a merchant in Harar. My father.'

For a few moments we were all silent. The silence was an African silence of stirring leaves and distant animal cries.

Way back in '42 I had often thought the easiest way out of the Jonnet problem would be for me to kill him or have him killed. I was glad in that moment that I had not done it. As the silence gradually fell apart and we talked again and sipped our coffee, Jonnet took Aliki to see a pet

71

cheetah that was tied to a sundial at the edge of the garden. He was talking to her. Earnestly and vigorously, and they looked incongruous in the pale moonlight. The tall, slim, elegant young girl and the portly, elderly man.

Peers and his wife talked the rubbish of their kind. The petty deeds and misdeeds of the London social climbers. Peers himself was distant and formal, but his wife was taken with the idea of me marrying Aliki. French though she was, she had been brought up in this overheated corner of Africa and the marriage was very much part of that scene. Out here it was natural and normal. Only in Europe would it be the subject of gossip. It looked as if under the tough exterior there was a touch of romance. Just as there was with her father. No doubt the gift of the jewelled cross had been calculated to smooth down any resentment I may have felt at his crude warning. And if bribe it was, it was all the more effective because it had been a gift for Aliki, not me. But it could easily have been some object of value that had no patina of long-ago love. But I recognized also the threat in the story he had told us.

Shortly after Aliki and Jonnet came back to the small circle, we said our thank yous and good-nights and they had stood waving to us as the car circled the driveway, to take us back to the hotel.

Back at the hotel there was a note to call Joe. I checked through our room carefully before I phoned. It had all the signs that it had been searched by a specialist, certainly a Russian not an Ethiopian. They had sliced open Aliki's perfumed soap but when they had put it back together again although there was no visible join line, the embossed name was slightly out of alignment. When you do this little trick you match the two cut halves under warm, running water and it's easy to miss checking the trademark, especially in a foreign language. I phoned the manager and asked for my photographic equipment to be taken out of the hotel safe. I spent ten minutes going over it carefully. I was pretty sure it hadn't been touched.

It was midnight before I was able to contact Joe. He came up to my room in dressing-gown and pyjamas. It was time we talked to Aliki, and it was time we made some plans. Aliki made us hot chocolate and we sat back in the deep chairs with our feet up on the low table, and the ceiling fan turning to cover our voices.

'You got anything special to tell us, Joe?'

'Very little. I think we should get cracking.'

'D'you want to put Aliki in the picture? I haven't told her anything.'

'Fine. Can I ask you something first, Aliki?'

'Of course.'

He pointed a foot in my direction. 'How much d'you care about this fella?'

Aliki didn't look at me. Her head bent as if she were praying, and then it came up as she looked at Joe. She spoke slowly and softly, as if the words were to be part of a legal document, or evidence in court.

'I care. I love. With all my heart and all my mind. To the end of my days, and one more.'

There was a moment's silence and then Joe put down his cup and shoved his hands in the pockets of his dressing-gown.

'I can see that I'll be fending for myself from now on. OK. Let's get on with it.' He sighed as he looked at Aliki. 'We think that the Russians have taken over here and that they're telling these boys that they can be running half of Africa if they just do as they're told. Kenya, Uganda, Mozambique, Somalia and Zambia. Are we right?'

'So far they talk only about Somalia and Kenya. They say about the Federation of East Africa to be ruled from Addis.'

'Do the Ethiopians believe them?'

'Not entirely, but they think that the Russians will have to do what they tell them to do. The Russians have made many opportunities to make them think this. There is maybe some decision to make where the Russians don't really care which way it goes, so at the start they take the

73

opposite view and then let the Ethiopians seem to get their way and that makes them feel they are in control.'

'Who's in charge on the Russian side?'

'Panov. He is KGB and reports to Moscow direct.'

'Tell us about him. What sort of man is he?'

And I realized I was going to hear Aliki's description of a man who had slept with her, and for almost the first time in my life I felt the frustrating anger of jealousy. Whatever she said of him, he was a man. A man who had had her. And both of us knew it. Aliki reached forward and put down her cup.

'He is about thirty-five or so. Trained in Moscow and he has specialized in subversion. The training and organization of guerrillas. He has had much experience in Cuba, Chile and Syria. He is married with two children and they live in Kiev. He is in charge of the operation here in Addis and has almost *carte blanche*. Certainly as far as money and training is concerned. But I think Moscow would have to give permission if he want to make big changes. And they will say him when any large-scale military action will start.'

'What kind of military action, Aliki?' Joe looked at her intently as he spoke.

'I think from something he said that Somalia would be taken over first.'

'Any indication how soon this would be?'

'Not really, but there were many arms brought into Massawa a month ago and I know there was a deadline.'

With great skill she'd made the man into a machine and it was easier now for me to join in.

'If I get some paper can we draw out a plan of the Russians' house?'

'Of course.'

We started with a plan of the house and then we drew separate sheets for individual rooms and the grounds. When we had finished it was obvious that the room that mattered was the room with the radio and the filing cabinets. Aliki said that the radio was manned twenty-four hours a day.

'What sort of cabinets are they? Wood or metal?'

She shook her head slowly. 'I can't remember, Johnny.'

'What colour are they, brown, grey, green?'

She shrugged. 'I've only been in that room two or three times. I just didn't notice.'

And with all that dreadful, inbuilt, feminine intuition that you've got if you were in the racket and survived, I worked it out. She'd been in there because Panov was on duty. He was having it off with her to pass the time away. The big man could break the rules. Just as he had when he attacked her in the corridor. I didn't look at her when I asked the question.

'Did Panov ever do radio duty?'

I didn't look at her but I could feel her looking at me. She knew I needn't have asked, because she knew that I already knew.

'Yes.'

Joe caught the falter, the sad inflection, in her voice. He looked sharply at her and then at me. He wasn't on the wavelength but he knew the atmosphere had changed.

I asked all the questions from then on. It was more like an interrogation. And as she strove desperately to answer and remember details I was ashamed of my attack, but I couldn't stop. It was nearly half an hour later, after an uncomplaining Aliki had answered patiently as if she were some criminal, that my jealous anger went as if it had been suddenly switched off. It was becoming clear that the emotional problems weren't all going to be Aliki's.

But by now I knew what we should be doing, and I guessed that Joe would have reached the same conclusion. I looked across at Aliki.

'D'you know anyone who can put us in touch with the top people in the Eritrean Liberation Movement?'

'I only know that they work very closely with the Somalis, I could make contact through them.' She shrugged. 'My connections are all with the Somalis. They're my people, not the Eritreans or the Ethiopians.'

Eritrea had been handed over to Addis Ababa by the

UN in 1952, and that had exacerbated the existing natural hatred of centuries. This was in the northern region of Ethiopia, and on the southern border the UN had given the wild nomadic Somali tribes of the Ogaden and their homeland to Addis in 1960; but all their ethnic, religious and historic ties were to Somalia. It might have all looked very tidy on the map, but in fact it had been a guarantee of a continuous guerrilla war that would inevitably end in open warfare. On the northern border that stage had already arrived.

'How long would it take, Aliki?'

'Tomorrow.'

Five minutes later we called it a day, and as he stood at the door Joe had looked back at us both.

'I think we should arrange a British passport for Aliki. What d'you think?'

Aliki looked at me. 'What do you want, Johnny?'

'It would give you more protection.'

She nodded and looked across at Joe.

'Yes, I think we do that.'

Aliki sat on the balcony looking at the new blue passport with Her Majesty's Consul's signature still fresh and shining black. She was admiring the photographs that I had taken and processed that morning. Joe had brought the passport back from the embassy himself, and on the official envelope it said, 'Welcome citizeness. J.S.' She had liked that. So had I.

She had spent an hour on the telephone and now we were awaiting a visitor.

Reception announced his arrival ten minutes later and we asked them to show him up.

Muhammed Issa was not what I expected. Like most Somalis he was tall and thin, but unlike most Somalis he wore a blue denim safari jacket and denim slacks. He shook hands with us both in turn and bowed politely to Aliki before making himself comfortable in one of the

76

armchairs. He took one of my cigarettes, and as he was waving out the match he looked up at me as he spoke.

'Miss Yassou asked me to come here to talk with you.' He leaned back comfortably. 'And here I am.'

It was Joe who led us off. 'This sort of talk can be dangerous for both parties, Mr Issa, so I'd like to suggest we all prove our good faith.'

Muhammed Issa smiled through the cigarette smoke. 'By all means, Mr Shapiro. How do we do that?'

'I suggest we go about it like this. We take it in turn to ask a question or two. If either side feels the other is lying or even dodging the issue they are entitled to walk out. We're either levelling or we're not. If we're not, we're wasting our time. Agreed?'

'Agreed. Do I get the first question?'

'If you wish.'

'Why are you and Mr Grant in Addis?' His eyes were on Joe's face but Joe didn't hesitate.

'We're interested in what the Russians are up to.'

Muhammed Issa smiled a wintry smile. 'Not a lie, Mr Shapiro, but far from levelling, as you call it. Any newspaper man, any diplomat is interested in what the Russians are up to in any part of the world. I think I am entitled to leave on the grounds that you are hedging, but your answer was at least not a lie. I suggest I ask a second question.'

Joe sat silently but didn't dissent.

'What, Mr Shapiro, do you *think* the Russians are up to?'

Joe took longer this time before he answered. 'We think they want to push the Ethiopians into taking over other East African countries – Somalia and Kenya for a start.'

Muhammed Issa nodded and waved his hand towards us. 'Your turn.'

'D'you think that what we suspect is right?'

'I think that many people share your fears.'

'I asked what you think. Not what many people think.'

Issa shrugged and smiled, and, as I was opening my

77

mouth to speak, I heard Aliki draw her breath sharply and she was speaking to the Somali in their own tongue. There was anger in her face and although I couldn't understand what she was saying it was obvious that Muhammed Issa was getting an earful of the Somali Riot Act. When Aliki finally came to a stop she turned to me.

'I told him to stop messing about. It is like children.'

For a moment we all sat there, then Issa shrugged and said, 'I think we could talk, Mr Shapiro. Let me be quite frank. I am a Somali, as you know, and my only direct interest is to prevent any action against my country.'

Joe nodded amiably, 'That's fair enough, Mr Issa, but I'm sure you'll understand that the only people doing anything active against the Ethiopians are the Eritreans in the north – in Asmara.'

'I understand you want to make contact with them through me.'

'That's it.'

'What do you want to know in particular?'

'About the Russian material at Massawa.'

The big brown eyes looked at the three of us and he was silent for almost a minute before he spoke. 'That's more the concern of my country than the Eritreans.'

Joe looked deadpan. 'How come? It's a long way from Massawa to Mogadishu.'

Muhammed Issa turned to Aliki and spoke to her in Somali. He seemed to be asking her a series of questions and it sounded as if she were trying to convince him of something. When they had finished he turned to Joe.

'Mr Shapiro, I've been explaining the position to Miss Yassou. We have a close liaison with the Eritrean guerrillas but we are both very occupied with our own country's problems. We consult, we exchange information, we have the same objectives, but that is all. The Russian weapons at Massawa are for use against Somalia so we were kept informed because of this. Most of that material is no longer in Massawa. It was taken by road convoy to the south.'

78

Joe's voice was very quiet. 'Where in the south?'

'We don't know exactly, but the convoys were seen outside Harar. Then they went along the escarpment road and all the roads towards the border were blocked off for two weeks.'

'Any ideas about what material was transported?'

'Most of it was in big cases but there were three big tracked vehicles that moved under their own power.'

'Can you describe them?'

Issa shook his head, 'No, but I can let you talk to men who actually saw them. They are only tribesmen so they know nothing about weapons except rifles, but they watched the convoys when the Eritreans told us they were on the way.'

'Where are these men?'

'They're from the border at Jigjiga. They sell skins and *ghee* in Harar.'

I asked him where we could contact him and he smiled. 'Miss Yassou can contact me. She knows how.'

I looked at Aliki, and she nodded.

We spent an hour after Issa had gone with the big maps that Joe had got from the embassy. They were the old Italian ones that I knew so well from my days in the Ogaden. Beautiful colours, beautiful printing, and utterly unreliable. They were apt to show rivers in the wrong places and the marked water-holes were no more than indications of Italian optimism. In a country of nomads the natives don't use maps, they know where the rivers are, and they and their flocks can smell water a day's trek away. But we weren't nomads and almost any maps were better than nothing.

High, rugged mountains curved round the city of Harar and the escarpment roads to the plains that led to the small dusty ramshackle town of Jigjiga were cut into the sides of the mountains so that their convolutions snaked above the river two thousand feet below. The frightening hairpin bends, and the vertiginous sight of the thin threads of the rivers made the journey a nightmare. When the rains came the route was virtually impassable. But down on the plains it was an ideal area to store weapons no matter how large or how many. Thousands of arid, empty, square miles of sand, rock and camelthorn. With little water, and not a cloud between you and a sun that looked and felt like an open-hearth furnace.

As I shoved my finger around the map and talked of Jigjiga, Hargeisha, Berbera and Daghabur it brought home to me Joe Shapiro's complete ignorance of the country. The huddle of mud huts at Jigjiga, the two buildings of Daghabur, the smaller about ten foot square where all those years ago I'd pulled rank to use it as my HQ for a couple of months. And my cornflakes and Nestlés milk being dropped by parachute from the Beech-craft that flew across the Red Sea from Aden. Hundreds of square miles that were so bereft of humans that the plane could pick out the white circle on the canvas top of my three-tonner wherever I might be on ration day.

Although I talked and described, I knew that there was no way to paint a useful picture for an inexperienced European. Just the names brought back for me those grim months and the desperate need after only a few days to belong somewhere, the urge to camp alongside some ant-hill that rose up in a vaguely familiar fountain of red sand. The absolute silence, no animals, no birds, just that wind that blew across the plains at sundown, no more than two feet from the ground but bringing down the temperature so that even inside the truck you slept under three blankets wearing your greatcoat.

Long after Joe had gone to his suite I sat on the bed and talked to Aliki, and it was clear to both of us that we were going to need some local help.

It would take us two days to cover Asmara if we went by plane, an extra day in Addis, then down to Dire Dawa and Harar at the end of the line, to make it look routine. Once in Harar we'd have to make up the words to suit the music.

8

I phoned the German who operated his Cessna out of the Addis airport and he stayed overnight with us while I photographed around Asmara. We kept well clear of all the local protesters, and just to keep the picture of innocence I phoned Ato Kebede to check that he didn't want me to photograph in Massawa. He didn't. Maybe some other time.

For the two days we were tailed around Asmara. There were at least six or seven on the team. We didn't play games with them, and we took it for granted that our rooms were bugged.

Back at the Hilton in Addis there was some mail for me, and on the flaps of the envelopes there were those telltale straight lines that showed they had been steamed and the flaps eased up with a knife. No matter if you're sharp enough to steam them again before you press down the flaps, you can never get those marks out completely. But you wouldn't notice them if you weren't looking for them.

There was a report from the studio. As usual they were doing better while I was away than we normally did when I was there. A four-page spread had been accepted by *Harper's* and, wonder of wonders, Saatchi & Saatchi had deigned to praise the photographs for the poster campaign. There was a second demand, the red one, from the Inland Revenue, and three envelopes marked personal for me. There was a querulous note from Daffers enclosing a cutting from *The Times* announcing her betrothal. A couple of full-frontal nudes from an eighteen-year-old blonde, with a stencilled letter stating that she was aiming to be next season's top model, and hinting at fantastic privileges for the photographer who made it all possible. I looked at the postmark and it was ten days old. They had probably drawn lots for her by now, because with those boobs and that grin she'd probably make it. The last letter was local, and it was from Logan Peers's wife. She would like to talk with me in private. Would I phone her discreetly.

I phoned the number she had given and she answered herself. Would I meet her at her father's office in the market square?

When I got there the clerk took me up the wooden steps to the first floor and at the end of a short corridor he opened the door to a large office. There was a big old-fashioned desk with its top inlaid with red leather. The walls were teak and bare, and there was a spread of four or five upright chairs and three deep leather armchairs. In one of which sat Sabine Peers.

As so often happened with French women in their colonies, she aped Paris in every way possible. The carefully swept-back hair swirled into an ornate chignon, and its deep black defied her age. The high cheekbones and the line of the jaw set off the wide mouth and the brown eyes. Her ears were mean and thin but the big gold earrings, tiny globes with an equator of diamonds, ensured that they would seldom be noticed. The Hermès scarf was knotted with that chic casualness that bespeaks great care, and the neat shoes were fashioned from some soft snakeskin that showed the shape of her toes. The fine jersey dress was biscuit and cream, and where its elegance touched her body it could have been skin. Her long legs were clad in what I was sure was silk rather than nylon, and I guessed that they were stockings not tights, and that the suspender belt would be white and frilly.

She waved me to the armchair facing her, and pointed her slim hand at the tray and the drinks.

'Whisky, gin or wine?'

'Maybe I could have one later.'

She nodded and carefully arranged the smooth shapely legs. There was no trace of coquettishness, she was arranging her limbs for comfort, nothing more.

'I'm glad you were able to come, Mr Grant, my father was much concerned that I should speak to you.' She paused, but I didn't speak, and she went on. 'My father has a strange sort of liking for you, and he feels that you're getting mixed up in things that maybe you don't understand.'

'I don't think he should worry, Mrs Peers. I can look after myself.'

She reached for a cigarette and fiddled with a gold lighter before she spoke again. She looked up at me. 'I'm not sure that that's true, Mr Grant.' And she had that knowing look that women adopt when they're quite sure they're going to drop a verbal bomb on you. The sort of look that mothers give their sons when they find that first copy of *Playboy* in the drawer under the balsawood and the model aeroplane plans. The look that stoats give rabbits. I patted the ball back carefully.

'What makes you think that, Mrs Peers?'

She put her head on one side as if considering how she could phrase the bad news.

'I made some inquiries in London, Mr Grant. A friend of mine is a friend of Daphne Partridge, and I gather that a Mr Shapiro was a friend of yours in London. You knew one another in the army, I understand. She thought he worked for the Ministry of Labour or some such thing. I think that if I mentioned this to my husband he would be able to check on Mr Shapiro through some of his old contacts from Queen Anne's Gate and Broadway. What do you think?'

'I think he's probably done that already, Mrs Peers.'

She shook her head briskly. 'No. I can assure you that he knows nothing about this at all. Neither does my father for that matter. Just you and me.'

The standard response to mothers is that *Snappy Stories*,

83

or *Playboy* or whatever, was given you by the lady at the bookshop in mistake for *Practical Aeromodelling*, or you are just keeping it for the boy next door. Both carry the seeds of destruction because the next question is 'What bookshop – the police should know', or 'Right, I shall go round and tell Mrs Mulroy what's going on. Disgusting.' There is no reply that doesn't add to the disaster. Silence in this situation is truly golden.

I heard myself saying, 'I think you should come to the point, Mrs Peers.'

Like Churchill, she was magnanimous in victory. 'I think you and I should decide what to do together.'

'Let's do that.'

She leaned back, and the faint smile was tactless but revealing. She loved the bit of power that was the prize for her curiosity about my background. I thought a little counterpunching was called for.

'What made you so interested in my background?'

She smiled and shrugged. 'I was brought up on you. Quite genuinely my father had respect for you. And apart from that you're an attractive man. I asked my friend to check on your attachments back in London. I think you had a lucky escape, I might say, from your Daffers. Doesn't sound your type at all.' And for the first time I sensed an underlying note of sexual interest.

'And why haven't you mentioned your news to your husband?'

Her eyebrows went up in scorn. 'Oh for God's sake, that *creature*. I use *him*, he doesn't use me. He belongs to my father. He earns his money by doing as he's told. Forget him.'

'I think you underrate him.'

Her nostrils widened and the pale face had red patches of anger. 'Not me, my friend. He wanted me from the moment he saw me, and when he found out who my father was he couldn't wait. It doesn't take much to make fifteen-year-olds open their legs, and when Papa caught us one night I knew from the look on his face that it wasn't an accident when he marched in. He knew all the time. Logan thought he was smart, banging the villain's daughter, but dear Papa was smarter. He'd let it happen, and just tied the final knots to suit himself. It suited them both. Logan got a millionaire's daughter and my father could do what he wanted without fear of arrest by the British. I hadn't known what Logan was, his job I mean, I thought I was being screwed for my fatal charm, and when I learned otherwise I didn't want to marry him. I yelled blue murder but Papa wasn't having any. It was marry Logan or out in the cold, cold, snow. Being my father's daughter I married him.'

'Even fools can be dangerous.'

'Of course. But if that bastard didn't toe the line, he'd be in real trouble. I'd see to that.'

'What's he doing out here anyway?'

'My father brought him out when he heard that you were coming. Just a piece of insurance.'

I didn't believe that that was all the story, but I didn't say so.

'And why haven't you given your news to your father?'

'For two reasons. If I tell him he would inevitably react violently against you, and that would be unwise. And secondly, I think you could influence my father against getting deeper into this situation.'

'What situation?'

She reached again for the cigarettes and took a long time with the lighter. As she exhaled the first smoke she looked across at me speculatively, weighing me up.

'The situation with the Russians and the Ethiopians. I think he's getting out of his depth.'

'Tell me.'

She stretched out the long, shapely legs and leaned back with her arm trailing almost to the floor as she flicked her cigarette. The brown eyes looked at me for long moments before she spoke.

'My father is a millionaire many times over. Always he

85

has made his money the hard way. He could have made it as a merchant. A lot of it has come that way. But there always had to be some risk in the background. That's why he played silly games with the Japanese. But if it wasn't them it was the Vichy French. Arms-smuggling, drug-smuggling, gold for the Indians, always something against the law. He is really a kind of white Ethiopian; we have houses all over East Africa but Addis is his home. He belongs here because he likes their wickedness. He is a wicked man himself. But I mean *wicked*, not evil. And what he is mixed up in now is evil. And it's not local, it's much bigger than that. He is an old man now, and this seems like a last adventure. He is making a lot of money from it, but in the end they will eat him. I would like you to be just a little bit on his side.'

'I think he would resent any comment from me.'

'But of course.' And she stood up, smoothing the dress over her hips as she looked at me. 'All I ask is that if it happens that it lies in your power you remember this meeting and you pay me back for saying nothing, by showing mercy to my father.'

'D'you ever see your brother these days?'

She frowned. 'You mean Jean-Luc?'

'Yes.'

'He lives in Paris.'

'And his wife, the Italian girl?'

She threw the cigarette impatiently away, and it lay smouldering on the brown tiles. She jerked round to face me, her face tight with anger.

'My God, you'd rather he was evil, wouldn't you? OK he screwed his pretty daughter-in-law, is that what you heard?'

I nodded.

'But you didn't hear that Jean-Luc wouldn't have touched her because he was a queer. And you didn't hear that my father never had a woman since my mother died when we were kids. And nobody ever thought that old man Jonnet actually loved the little Italian girl? So what?

He screwed her, and he found some peace with her, and she with him, and Jean-Luc didn't give a damn.'

She was breathless from her tirade but her anger had dissipated as she spoke. She shrugged. 'And how the hell could you have known?' She grinned, a bit like her old man. 'How about something to eat? *J'ai vachement faim.*' And that was the only real French I'd ever heard her speak.

There were meats and salad under damp white cloths, and we ate looking out at the market. And finally she said, 'Do you agree that my saying nothing entitles me to ask consideration for my father?'

'It wasn't necessary.'

She looked surprised and slightly aggressive. 'Why not?'

'Because of the little gold cross he gave to Aliki.'

Her mouth opened and she frowned for a moment as she thought. Then her face relaxed and she smiled. A genuine smile. 'My God, another romantic.' But she was relaxed now, and she walked down to the street with me and called the driver to take me back to the hotel. Not my kind of woman, but better than Logan Peers deserved.

Joe was a long time silent when I gave him the news and then he leaned back with his eyes closed; they stayed closed when he said, 'So what do we do now, my boy?'

'You go back to London, Joe. There's really no choice.'

He sat up in the chair, his pale blue eyes looking at me. 'Yes. With me out of the way you'd have a clean run, and I'll keep the embassy here toeing the line so that you get the support you need.'

'I need more money. I need a radio, and I'm going to need weapons.'

'That'll be no problem, and it will be easier with London putting pressure on the embassy. Is there anything else?'

'Yes.' I said. 'You've got to keep up the tourist bit. Keep in touch with Ato Kebede. Get a small para in the

87

nationals at home about my trip here. I'm probably going to need some specialist help and I'll need it quick. Maybe a radio operator. I shan't know till I'm nearer the target.'

Joe stood up. 'OK. Let's set a reasonable brief.' He paused. 'We'd like to know where this arms dump is, what it consists of, and if it's operational. No fancy stuff. OK?'

We went to the airport to wave goodbye to Joe, and as we stood by the windows at the airport the late sun was on his battered face as he turned towards me. 'You know this whole thing is bloody ridiculous. You and a pretty girl against this lot. We must be out of our minds.'

'We're only having a look around, Joe. We're not starting a fight.'

He nodded and pursed his lips. 'You just keep it that way, my boy.'

'I can look after myself, don't worry.'

'There's Aliki as well, remember.'

'Oh, I can look after my pretty wog all right.'

Joe looked scandalized and offended, and he turned away impatiently. 'Don't use words like that, Johnny. It's outrageous.'

And then he caught sight of Aliki's grin and looked even more offended.

9

As I drove us back to the Hilton Aliki sat silently beside me. Finally she spoke. 'He is a good man that Joe. He likes you like a son.'

'We'll have him as the bride's father at our wedding.'

She sighed. 'I hope it happens to us. The wedding.' She turned to look at me. 'Are you a Christian?'

'More or less. How about you?'

'Momma was Greek Orthodox, Papa was Muslim.'

'Which do you fancy?'

'I will be whatever you wish.'

'How soon can we see Issa again?'

'Two hours. Maybe sooner.'

'Has he got transport?'

'Yes.'

'Tell him to meet us at Biffi's place at Bishoftu at four o'clock.'

'OK. I phone him from hotel.'

'Can you contact him without phoning?'

'You think they bug our room?'

'I'm sure they have. Can you send a message to him?'

'Yes, of course.'

'How?'

'There is a Somali at the hotel. A cleaner. She will go for me.'

'Is it OK for you to go to Mogadishu?'

'Of course. I am born there.'

'What about me?'

'Foreigners are not welcome. Maybe Americans are OK but not others.'

'Are there any Russians still there?'

'Very few. They were all kicked out when the Russians started supporting the Ethiopians. Just diplomats.'

'Do they have any influence?'

'A little, but not in official circles. They are hated by the government.'

'Are there planes? Civilian planes?'

'I don't know. I would think so. We have a civilian airline.'

'D'you know something?'

She turned her head quickly, her eyes concerned. 'What?'

'I love you.'

She sighed a deep sigh. 'Why now that you say it?'

'I thought you might like it.'

She smiled. 'I do but you sounded so serious when you say if I know something. I thought it was going to be something bad.'

'Not with me, my love.'

'What are we going to do, Johnny?'

'We're going to talk with Issa. I'm going to hire a vehicle and camping gear. We're going to wait for the radio and a message from Joe. And then . . . well, we'll see what we can do.'

'Are you scared?'

'Of what?'

'Of what the *derg* or the Russians might do to you.'

'Why should they do anything to me? I'm not going to do them any harm.'

'You're going to spy on them.'

I smiled. 'We're just going to cast our eyes around a bit. Just an intelligent glance here and there.'

'And Jonnet?'

'What about him?'

'He is as dangerous as the Russians.'

'Maybe. Don't worry about him, though.'

But I thought then that I ought to send her back to London. It was stupid and unfair to have her with me. But

90

I was almost as scared to send her back as to keep her with me. I had already realized that I hated to think of her in England on her own. The insults and humiliation from the moment she arrived. It was a salutary thought that there were Englishmen who would delight in harassing her with all the obscenities and filth that went with colour prejudice. Her beauty would be no protection. Maybe even an additional provocation. For the first time in my life I actively disliked my countrymen. It was easy enough to disapprove and despise the racialists in theory, but to have somebody you loved on the receiving end of that rabid mob made you realize what it was really all about. Some lout could call my beautiful Aliki a 'black bastard' and nobody would give a damn. The Immigration people could ask her if she was a virgin and subject her to a body search without a second's thought. I had not much liked the fact that these things went on but I'd never done anything about it. It angered me that it left me no real choice and that she would have to run the risks that went with staying with me. What angered me even more was that what I was doing was as much for the benefit of the racist louts as for ordinary decent people.

Back at the Hilton I packed my gear, booked us on the early-morning train to Dire Dawa and arranged for a hire car for the journey to Harar.

Issa couldn't make it that evening so we fixed a meeting for two days' time in Harar. I was looking forward to seeing Harar again. I'd lived there for three months after the Emperor had thrown me out of Addis. Harar had still been controlled by the British.

The railway line from Addis to Jibuti had been kept in good repair after the war and the journey down to Dire Dawa was boring but comfortable. I shot a dozen rolls of Ektachrome using Aliki as my model and we left early the next morning for the drive down to Harar.

It doesn't look far on a map but on the ground it is

91

horrific. Winding escarpment roads with hundreds of hairpin bends and a sheer drop of four or five thousand feet down steep mountainsides. Scores of British army trucks had ended their days in the wide river below that looked like a thin cotton thread. If you met a vehicle coming from the other direction you had to ease your way past a few inches at a time. Nobody tried the journey at night unless they were desperate. I had done the journey dozens of times in the old days but the road was even worse now from years of neglect. Addis officials made the journey by plane.

As we went past Lake Aramiya it was almost like coming home and I could see the villa I once lived in up on the hillside just as we turned towards the city.

In size you couldn't really class Harar as a city. But in dignity and history it was there long before London, Rome and Paris. It's a walled city that has been ruled by Arabs, Egyptians, Somalis and Ethiopians. Haile Selassie was born there. The home of Somalis, Amharas, Hararis and Gallas. A population of about twenty-five thousand and the trading centre for coffee, durra, skins and local drugs. There was one main street that the Italians had built.

There was one hotel. It had been there before the war. The Italians had built it and the Ethiopians had miraculously kept it in decent condition. It had been a depressing sight after the Italian surrender to see beautiful buildings slowly disintegrating after the looting. Donkeys and goats clattering over marble and mosaic floors.

I spent the morning taking shots of Aliki in the market looking at the crude but beautiful gold jewellery and rings. In the afternoon I took her across the wide street to see what had once been the Duke of Aosta's official residence. After the capitulation it had been the headquarters and mess of the British Commander and Twelfth South African Division.

I couldn't recall the general's name but he was a big burly man with a cloud of white hair and demanding habits. Night after night he lay back in the Duke's magnificent marble bath in a cloud of steam yelling 'Louder, louder' as I read him the day's reports from the brigades. I told Aliki a little about those days before she was born.

'My mother said you wrote to her several times after you left Addis. Why did you write to her?'

'I liked her. She was special. And she was kind to me.'

'How was she kind?'

'She cared about whether I was happy or sad. She took risks to help me. She was on my side.'

'Did you think she was pretty?'

'I thought she was beautiful. And she was.'

'But you never slept with her. Why not?'

'It wasn't that sort of relationship. She had plenty of men friends. I assumed that she was already fixed up so far as bed was concerned.' I smiled. 'Anyway I wasn't sure that she would have said yes.'

Aliki smiled. 'Maybe if she'd said yes you would have been my father.'

'Then I'm glad I didn't ask.'

'There's Issa going into the hotel.'

'OK. Let's go back.'

Way back in wartime I'd been able to get my small Fiat up the winding path to the house but the path was rutted and potholed now. But the house looked much the same except that the bougainvillaea had now covered it completely. Across the roof and over the veranda the mauve and pink bracts dazzled the eye.

As I stood looking, halfway up the path, Aliki said, 'Why don't we walk up?'

'Would you mind?'

She laughed, took my hand and led the way. It looked much smaller now as we stood on the veranda. The slatted door hung from one hinge and a bird flew out as we walked inside. And as we stood there it seemed only weeks since it had been my home. Mine and Paynter's.

'Why did you like it so much, Johnny?'

'I don't really know. I just seemed at home here. Nothing bad happened while I lived here. And I rather liked Paynter who lived here with me.'

'Who was he?'

'He was about forty then. A major. We used to talk about what we'd do after the war. He only wanted one thing and that was to live for the rest of his life in Saigon. He said it was the most beautiful place in the world. I'd no idea where it was and I don't think I ever thought about it again until the Vietnam war. And I wondered if Paynter had made it and what had happened to him. He was a strange man. Always calm and relaxed. I asked him what he was going to do in Saigon. I meant how would he earn a living. He just smiled and said that being there was the only thing that mattered.'

'How long were you here?'

'Only a few months. Two or three. Then I went down to Mogadishu.' I turned towards the doorway. 'Let's sit on the steps. There's a marvellous view across to the lake.'

As we sat there looking towards the town I could remember Paynter putting on the record again and again on our wind-up portable gramophone. It was always Josephine Baker singing *La Petite Tonkinoise*. He put it on as soon as he woke, and it was the last thing he played at night. I'd pinched an almost new copy of it for him from the German Armistice Commission's mess when we eventually took Jibuti. You'd have thought I'd given him a gold bar he was so pleased.

I turned to Aliki. 'What time will Issa be coming again?'

'He just said evening.'

'Who knows more about the *derg* and Addis, you or him?'

'I think I do. But he knows more about what's going on in Somalia than I do.'

'Tell me about the *derg*. Why's it called that anyway?'

'It's an Amharic word. It just means a group, a committee. It's always used as if it was a military thing. Like

94

junta. But it's just an accident that the committee grew out of the army.'

'How did the Russians get them to start the revolution?'

'They didn't. The Russians weren't even in Addis except for their embassy people. The revolution was home-grown.'

'Tell me about it.'

'Well, you know from your time in Addis that the Emperor and the aristocracy ruled the country in their own interests.' Aliki turned to look at me, smiling. 'Do you know who really brought the Emperor down?'

'No. Tell me.'

'It sounds crazy but it was the taxi drivers of Addis.'

'You're kidding.'

She laughed. 'I'm not. There was a small mutiny at the army garrison in Neghele in mid-January 1974. The Emperor sent investigators down and the soldiers just imprisoned them. People suddenly saw that the Emperor wasn't all powerful. He *could* be defied.

'In February there were big demonstrations in Addis by students and teachers. There were mutinies at a number of army units and then the taxi drivers struck because of a huge rise in the cost of petrol because of OPEC. The government was replaced by the Emperor and he made substantial political and economic concessions. And there were no punishments.

'All the army were outraged by the corruption in all parts of government. It wasn't political nor inflamed from outside. Then the Second and Fourth Army Divisions in Addis revolted and out of that came the *derg*. They had two vice-chairmen. The junior one was Haile-Mariam Mengistu. And now he's ruling Ethiopia.'

'What happened to the Emperor?'

'A group of officers went to the Palace, arrested him and took him away. I saw him actually go. It was unbelievable. There he was, the King of Kings, the Lion of Judah, sitting as a prisoner in the back seat of a Volkswagen. Just a tiny little man with big brown eyes.'

She turned and looked at me. 'How did you get on with him?'

I shrugged. 'Quite well. He was a cunning little man. Nobody got really close to him. He was always very conscious of being the King of Kings and Lion of Judah.'

'What else can I tell you?'

'When did the Russians come in?'

'Mengistu used the words "socialist revolution" in his earliest speeches. He was invited to Moscow and it's obvious that they decided to back him. After he came back the mass killings of any kind of opponents increased fantastically. And after the Russians set up the mission here with hundreds of so-called advisers, weapons and aircraft just poured in. And slowly the Russians are taking over. And now the Cubans are coming in too. Not many, but there'll be plenty more before long.'

'Has the *derg* done any good for the people?'

'They've made it worse. D'you know what the average income was last year?'

'I've no idea.'

'A hundred and twenty US dollars a year.'

'What are the Russians aiming to do?'

'Just what you and Joe think they're going to do. They're encouraging Mengistu to think he can take over the whole of East Africa.'

'Do you think he could?'

'I'm sure he could if the Russians virtually do it for him.'

'And what do the Russians get out of it?'

'Oh Johnny. You don't need me to tell you that. Control of the Canal. Control of the Indian Ocean. All that would be left for them to take would be Japan and Australia. Another ten years maybe?'

'Let's go, honey. It's getting cool.'

As I stood up I could see the walls of the city of Harar. The city was straight out of the Bible. There was a camel train waiting outside the city gates. The gates were closed every night at sunset. They had closed every night for at least the last two thousand years. After sunset the camel trains had to camp outside for the night, but if you were a solitary traveller there was a narrow archway in the city walls just wide enough to take a single lean camel. These narrow archways existed all over the Middle East when towns were still walled. And everywhere they were called the 'needles eyes'. The biblical eye of a needle that is easier for a camel to pass through than for a rich man to enter the Kingdom of Heaven.

The early evening breeze had dropped and as we sat under the lights in the hotel garden it was clammily hot. We were finishing our coffee when Issa arrived. He nodded to Aliki then me as he pulled out a chair and drew up to the table.

'I've found a jeep you can hire and a tent. There's a trailer you can hire too if you want it.'

'It would be useful for petrol and water cans. Is it expensive?'

He shrugged. 'Why worry? It will go on your photographic expenses, won't it?'

'Sure. But if I behave like money's no object they'll maybe draw the wrong conclusions. Or the right ones.'

'Are you going to help us?'

'Who's "us"?'

'The Somalis.'

'Help in what way?'

'Help us against the *derg*. Help us to get back our territory – the Ogaden.'

'How can one man help you do that?'

'You can influence your government. The Russians in Addis are arming our enemies against us. Your government could stop them. It is in their interests to do so.'

'I'm just an ordinary civilian, Mr Issa. I have no influence with any government. I can only help you by exposing the Russians' arms build-up.'

'We can help you do that.'

'How?'

'We can show you their arms dump but we are not

97

sophisticated enough to identify the weapons and the vehicles. You could do that.'

'What help can you give?'

'Guides, trackers, soldiers, vehicles, supplies. Some protection maybe.'

'Let's be specific. Who is the "we" who can do this?'

'The SRC. The Supreme Revolutionary Council. And the Western Somalia Liberation Front. The leader of the WSLF has already confirmed to me that he will provide all the help you need. Anything. Money, lives, weapons. He has great respect for you.'

'How can he know anything about me? Good or bad.'

'I only tell you the message I got from him from his headquarters in Daghabur.'

'Can I meet him?'

'Not in Ethiopia. He would be recognized. He would meet you any time anywhere in Somalia.'

'Where are the arms?'

'Some are at Massawa in Eritrea. You already know about those. So do the Americans. But there are bigger dumps just outside Jigjiga. Only twenty kilometres from the Somali border. Nobody knows about those.'

'You have people who could take me there?'

'Yes, of course.'

'I'll have to spend two days photographing in Harar and Dire Dawa and then we'll be going back to Addis. Can I see you there?'

'I'll meet you anywhere you want, any time.'

10

After we had booked back in at the Hilton I took a taxi to the embassy. I was obviously *persona non grata* but they took me along to the Third Secretary's office.

He was young and smooth and well used to dealing with the embassy's unwelcome guests. He wasn't MI6 but he was used for liaison on intelligence matters with London. He waved me elegantly to a chair.

'How's the assignment going, Mr Grant?' He smiled. 'The photography.'

'Quite well, thank you. Any messages for me from London?'

'Ah yes,' he said languidly, 'London. I've got a box for you. Came in the bag. Very heavy. A cine camera I should think.' He smiled. 'Or maybe a radio.' He shrugged and laughed. 'I've arranged for one of our signals chaps to go over it with you. He says it's the very latest. Full of good things. And it's what he calls user-friendly. I gather that means that it's very easy to use.'

'Any messages?'

He reached into a drawer and pulled out several sheets of computer print-out. 'It'll take some time for you to absorb it. I've arranged a private office for you.' He paused. 'You'll see reference to a weapon. His Excellency has an aversion to weapons on diplomatic premises. I've taken the liberty of removing it, and the ammo, to my place. I'll be happy to hand it over whenever you wish. Quietly and discreetly, of course.'

'What is it?'

'I believe they're called Kalashnikovs.'

'I'd like the embassy to get me a pass to go down to Jigjiga in a few days' time.'

'Oh, my dear. His Excellency won't like that. Frowns all round, I fear. I think he will say that as you're working for our black friends they should be happy to supply that themselves.'

'Can you get me a jeep and some camping gear?'

'You mean a real jeep? The old-fashioned things or do you mean a Land-Rover?'

'Either, as long as it's in good running order.'

'I'll see what I can do. Leave it to me and I'll contact you early tomorrow.' He shrugged. 'Camping gear we can supply from our own stores. Is your friend going with you?'

'Yes. Miss Yassou will be with me.'

'A very beautiful girl, Mr Grant. Although the embassy has been worried about some of her friends in the past.' He hesitated and then saw the look in my eye. 'But of course in your good care there are no problems.'

'Is there a secure line to London?'

'Our London or your London?'

'My London.'

'Yes of course. But we have to alert them an hour ahead. You're welcome to use it.'

'Thanks.' I picked up the sheets of print-out. 'Can you show me the office I can use?'

It was a small office with a teak desk, a couple of chairs, a scrambler phone and an ordinary phone, a metal filing cabinet and no windows. It was next to the radio room and I could just hear the clatter of a teleprinter.

It took twenty minutes to read and absorb Joe Shapiro's piece. London had heard that whole squads of Cubans were coming in on troopships through Massawa. What had been treated as a problem was now being looked at as a threat. They had heard rumours that the supplies at Massawa were only intended for use by the *derg* against the dissidents in Eritrea and that there were other supply dumps being built up to roll back the Somali irregulars in the Ogaden. It was feared that the guerrilla action in the Ogaden would be used as an excuse to push on and take over the whole of Somalia. They wanted all the information I could get on the second build-up of supply dumps. They were prepared to send money through Mogadishu and to ask unofficially for the Somali government to cooperate with me. But there was the usual warning that if anything went wrong there was no question of official help and any connection with me would be denied. There was a list of five wavelengths that would be permanently manned, and it was emphasized that all I was asked to do was identify the site of the arms dump and if possible identify the weapons available. I was to take no action of any kind.

It was about what I could have expected but it angered me all the same. I wasn't in MI6 any more. I was a civilian. And out of a long-standing friendship with Joe Shapiro I'd let myself be talked into doing a mild bit of snooping for him and London. And all of a sudden I was getting orders. Orders that went far beyond what I'd volunteered to do. But unfortunately I knew that what Joe Shapiro had said was true. They had nobody to call on who had even heard of the Ogaden let alone lived there. There were probably not more than three other Europeans who knew the area at all in any real sense. One was an elderly sociologist at the London School of Economics, one was an invalid in California and the third was a civil servant in Auckland, New Zealand.

I wrote out a reply for the cipher clerk and then scrapped it to write another and another. The first was an angry refusal to do anything, and notification that I was taking the next flight available back to London with Aliki. The fifth and final message said that I would cooperate only in obtaining information. There would be no physical reconnaissance. And that I expected full protection from London for both Aliki and myself. It was cold and formal and sensible. And I wished that it had been angry and abusive and that I'd told them to get stuffed. I owed

101

Shapiro quite a lot from the old days but Aliki owed him nothing. But I was depressingly aware that it was Aliki's people who would benefit from whatever I could do.

Then Matthews, the Third Secretary, knocked and came in. 'All OK? Everything understood?'

I opened my mouth and then closed it. Why the hell should I let him know how I felt? I handed him the message. He read it briefly and then looked at me, half smiling.

'What the diplomats call a frank and free discussion of the issues at stake, eh?'

'How about you wheel in the radio expert.'

'Of course. Let me get rid of this first, then we'll go along to my office and he can tell you all about Single Side Band and MOSFET gates and all that. I love their electronic jargon, don't you?'

He picked up the print-out and my torn-up replies. 'Into the shredder with these, I think.'

The radio looked complex but it wasn't. It was Japanese and high technology and you didn't repair anything, you just shoved in a spare printed-circuit board and carried on. It was remarkably small for what it did but it weighed like lead. It worked off any one of three mains supplies and 6 and 12 volt DC.

I went back to the hotel and walked Aliki down to the swimming pool to make sure we weren't bugged as I told her more or less what Joe's message had said. She made little comment but I sensed that, unlike me, she was pleased at London's interest in the fate of her countrymen. It looked like I'd fallen in love with an Amazon.

102

11

Despite his languid attitude Matthews at the embassy did his stuff. He found me a Land-Rover in good condition with a trailer, and jerry-cans from the embassy stores. The Land-Rover had a small communications radio already fitted for safaris, and its aerial would be helpful and explainable. And with the vehicle that Issa was hiring we at least had back-up transport.

I took Aliki down to the *magalla* to give an Indian carpenter the dimensions of the wooden boxes I wanted him to make. I needed seven of various sizes for food and clothes and the bits and pieces that make camping comfortable. Only amateurs think that camping means roughing it. He promised them for that evening and Indian *fundis* keep their promises. They would not only be ready but beautifully made.

Back at the Hilton I asked the operator to get me put through to Ato Kebede. He was in a meeting but his deputy listened to my request for a permit to go down to Jigjiga. I told him that I needed shots away from the mountains and away from buildings and towns. He was noncommittal but said he would come back to me later.

It was less than twenty minutes when he phoned back and said that a permit for the journey there and back plus four days in Jigjiga was on its way to the hotel. It had been signed by Ato Kebede himself.

We were getting dressed for dinner when there was a knock on the door. When I opened it Jonnet was standing there.

'They said they had a permit for you. I offered to bring it as I was passing the hotel.'

I ushered him in, pointed to an armchair and offered him a drink. He shrugged. 'A Perrier water would be fine.'

I laughed. 'Is that one of your agencies?'

He smiled. 'I have an indirect interest, yes. I also have an unhappy liver.'

As I handed him the glass and sat down he raised his glass. '*A la vôtre, Monsieur Grant.*'

I raised my glass too. 'The same to you.'

'And your beautiful fiancée, how is she?'

'She's fine. She'll be out in a moment. We've suddenly realized that we're hungry.'

'Where are you eating?'

'Downstairs, in the hotel.'

'Could I persuade you to eat with me instead?'

'Let me ask Aliki.'

As I got up he turned to look at me. 'Even millionaires and villains get lonely when they're old.'

After that there was no way we could refuse and half an hour later the *maitre d'* showed the three of us to a table in an alcove and, gilding the lily, he not only took our order but served us himself. When we were at the coffee stage, Jonnet looked across at me and said softly, 'There is no chance I suppose that you would take advice from an old man?'

'About what?'

He sighed. 'I think you know, Mr Grant. It would be very very foolish.'

'What would be?'

'Your trip to Jigjiga.'

'Who said anything about a trip to Jigjiga?'

He shook his head slowly. 'I brought you the permit from the *derg*, and the embassy have hired a Land-Rover for you. And asked for a towbar for a trailer to be fitted.'

'Who told you that?'

'They hired it from me, Mr Grant. I have the only Land-Rover in Addis not owned by the army.'

'So why is my trip so foolish?'

'Do we have to play games?'

'Maybe. I don't know. You tell me.'

'I think that you and your colleague, Mr Shapiro, have probably successfully deceived the Ethiopians but I doubt if you have deceived the Russians.'

'Deceived them about what?'

Jonnet shrugged. 'The Russians will be watching you. You can be sure of that.'

'What are you trying to tell me, Jonnet?'

Jonnet turned to look at Aliki. 'Can't you tell him, Aliki? Tell him what they are like.'

I interrupted. 'I know what they're like, Jonnet. Just get it into your head that I'm taking photographs for a travel brochure. Don't make wild guesses about anything else.'

'You're being a fool, my friend. You should take this girl back to London on the first flight you can get. Forget Addis and all our machinations.' He paused and said quietly, 'forget Mogadishu too. It's a lost cause. It was a lost cause once the Russians arrived in Addis. When Moscow says the word it will be as good as finished. And if you don't take my advice you'll be dead before it's even started. Both of you.'

'Why are you so concerned about me, Jonnet?'

He looked away from me, across the dining-room, and then he looked back. First at Aliki and then at me.

'I don't really know. Maybe it's just that it seems such a waste of two people. Two nice people.' He hesitated and then went on. 'Let me tell you something. When the Russians first came here they needed help on all sorts of things. Who to contact. Who to ignore. How to go about their business without causing resentment. They turned to me. I was impressed by my talks with them. They were people who knew exactly what they wanted to do. Pragmatists. There was an excitement for me in being in their confidence. Not entirely in their confidence maybe, but enough for me to understand their reasoning.' He looked at Aliki. 'Your people were equally impressed. It was a mistake on the Russians' part to back Somalia. They recognized it quickly.' He shrugged. 'And we all know the outcome. Your people threw them out, and looked to the Americans. But the Americans don't understand Europeans let alone Africans, so you quarrel with the Americans even while they negotiate with you.

'But that's all in the past. So, like I say, I was impressed by the Russians' single-mindedness. Their ability to absorb and learn. Their energy. I'm still impressed. But I'm scared too. The *derg* is no longer its own master. They owe tens of millions of dollars to Moscow, but Moscow trades the debt for power and control. The *derg* are Moscow's puppets. I'm not sure that they recognize this and it will be a bitter blow when they do. But then it will be too late. Moscow will control the whole of East Africa. Every inch of it. You understand what I'm saying?'

I nodded and he went on. 'You are like a matchstick being swept over Niagara Falls. Don't get involved, I beg of you.'

'Thanks for the explanation and the warning. I'm sure you mean us well.' I smiled. 'I'll send you some nice colour prints of Jigjiga you can frame when I'm back in London.'

Jonnet turned, half smiling, shrugging helplessly as he looked at Aliki. 'I must leave you.' He waved for the bill and signed it without even glancing at it as he stood up. His hand touched my shoulder. '*Bonsoir. Soyez sage.*'

I started loading the Land-Rover and the trailer at eight the next morning and it took almost two hours. I took a few shots of Aliki at the wheel and then we got on our way.

It is about three hundred miles to Jigjiga if you measure it out on the map. On the ground it is well over five hundred and most of it is very rough going after Dire Dawa. It took us four days to get to Harar. We camped by the lake and avoided the city until the following morning when I took on petrol and water. We were on the escarpment roads by mid-morning and suddenly it was

106

Africa. Real Africa. Brown, arid and magnificent. Lonely and silent.

We camped that evening at a rock-face I knew where we came down from the mountains to the flat land on the approach to Jigjiga. As I set up the tent I pointed to the cliff.

'As soon as the sun goes behind the rocks over there you'll see a whole colony of baboons. I used to camp here just to see them.'

Aliki smiled. 'It's crazy that you know these places so well and they're my country, not yours.'

'There's another fifty miles before we get to your country, honey. Have you ever been to Hargeisha?'

'No. Tell me what it's like.'

'Get those sausages cooked and I'll tell you while we're eating.'

And then she was pointing. The cliff was swarming with baboon families. Babies clinging to their mothers' fur. Old males keeping guard on the rocks and even that far away the noise was incredible. The baboon colony had lived there for hundreds of years and at the foot of the rock-face was a small colony of colobus monkeys. You could see their sad black and white hides made into handbags and shoes in the Addis *magalla* and the tourist shops way down south in Nairobi.

When I'd spent those months on my own in the Ogaden I'd hated it. The loneliness, the constant dysentery, continuously on the move like the Somali nomads I was arming against the Emperor. But now with Aliki it was different. And all those lonely days suddenly seemed worthwhile.

'What are you thinking of?' she said softly.

'I was thinking about when I was here before in wartime.'

'What were you doing here?'

'I operated out of Mogadishu. Organizing parachute drops of rifles and ammunition for the Somali tribesmen. Showing them how to use the rifles and which way to point them.'

'And which way was that?'

'In the general direction of Ethiopia.'

'Was this because they threw you out?'

I laughed. 'I'm afraid not. It was official policy to teach the Emperor a lesson. We thought he was playing games with the Japanese and a border war might keep him occupied.'

'And did it?'

'I've no idea. I was taken away before it was possible to judge the results.' I grinned. 'But the Somalis loved it.'

'They won't love it when they're fighting the Cubans and the Russians.'

'You're right. It was a stupid thing to say. I guess life was a lot simpler in those days.'

'Will your people in London really do something to help us?'

'It's hard to say. They seem pretty worried about what's going on down here.'

'What can they do?'

'I don't know.'

'Issa doesn't like the British. He thinks they are worse than the Italians.'

'What doesn't he like about us?'

'He says you break any promise if it suits you.'

'How about we go to bed. I've put the sleeping-bag in the Land-Rover. It's going to be cold by midnight.'

It was cold long before midnight and despite the blankets piled on top of us it was one o'clock before I slept.

It seemed only a few minutes later when the noise awoke me. I slid out of the bag, crawled to the tailboard and pulled back the canvas flaps. It was just getting light and the noise was the clatter of a helicopter's rotors.

As I climbed out of the back of the Land-Rover I could see the chopper turning and banking and I could see a man in olive uniform in the passenger seat, his binoculars trained on us. There were no markings on the chopper but it didn't need any. It was a Polish Kania PZL. The Poles had tried to flog it in the USA as a civil helicopter. It was a general-purpose machine for carrying passengers or freight and the Soviet Union had given Warsaw an order for a hundred or so just to keep them happy. But what was interesting was that it only had a range of three hundred miles so it hadn't come from Addis.

I waved up at them amiably but they didn't respond. They circled us twice more and then flew off lazily to the south-east.

Aliki was still asleep when I looked inside the back of the Land-Rover. I started the small gas-burner, brewed up some tea, and fried a few eggs before I woke her.

As we ate it was as if the world had been switched off. There was complete silence. Not even the sound of a bird or an animal, and as far as you could see to the east was mile after mile of sand shimmering from the heat of the sun.

We were in no hurry and I checked on the contents of all the boxes. When I came to the radio I decided that I'd give it a trial run. They'd given me a codename to use – 'Crusader'. I took the leads to the spare battery and switched on. There was a Morse key in a foam container and I plugged it into the front panel of the transceiver. The red light came on as I turned the switch to transmit. I tapped out the codeword and confirmation that I was going to test the five frequencies in turn. Despite the shade inside the Land-Rover and the light foam head-phones sweat was pouring down from my forehead. They responded immediately on each of the frequencies in turn and I confirmed that the second and third frequencies were strongest and clear of static. I gave them my location and a nil report and closed down.

As I turned from the radio Aliki was standing there naked in the sun, sponging water over her shoulders, intent on what she was doing. She was so young and so beautiful, her flesh satin smooth and firm. She was like some beautiful animal. A gazelle. So right for her environment, so alive and vital, so unconcerned with her beauty. As I looked she turned and smiled at me. Smiled with those white white teeth. And I wanted to have her but it wasn't appropriate or timely. The smile was affection not invitation. And we had other things to do.

We rolled into Jigjiga at noon in a cloud of flies and dust. When I knew it, it was just a cluster of shacks made out of flattened petrol cans, corrugated iron and wattles and mud. There had been two cement buildings used by the governor and customs and excise men. What had once been not much more than a shanty town had been transformed into what looked like a prosperous market town. There were four long rows of houses and shops and a dozen administrative buildings.

I went the rounds and made my mark at the regional governor's office, at the police station, customs and excise and finally at the guardroom of the local garrison commander. They weren't used to dealing with foreigners, nor strange documents from Addis, but they all recognized Ato Kebede's signature when they saw it. I put the word out that I should be buying stores and petrol but that we should be camping outside the town at nights. Nobody was either interested or impressed by the news, but one and all were interested in Aliki. There was a lot of chatting-up in Somali and Amharic and Aliki smiled impartially on all and sundry.

I waited until late afternoon before I took any shots. The daytime sun would have made the shadows too harsh. I photographed her with the various local officials using the Polaroid back so that I could hand out prints to all concerned. It was not much more than a PR exercise but it seemed to work.

I saw Issa standing by an old Lancia Aprillia drawn up in the shadow of a *duka* selling iced drinks. When I looked at him again he nodded imperceptibly before he slid into the driver's seat and backed the car into the wide main street.

About an hour before sunset I headed back for the foot of the mountains. Issa was already there, his car parked under an outcrop of rock. You wouldn't be able to see it from the air. That was the plus. The minus was a train of twenty or more camels and a dozen men. Some of the camels were already lying down and you don't let camels settle down unless you mean to stay. It's a hell of a job persuading a comfortable camel to lurch to its feet. Issa was talking to three of the men. They had their cotton *shammas* draped over their heads and it was impossible to tell what tribe they were from.

I stopped at our previous night's site and started unpacking the food for our evening meal. After it got dark I could see the camelmen's fire and could hear the soft sounds of their voices.

We were almost ready to turn in when Issa loomed out of the darkness and sat himself down beside me.

'I want you to meet the man, Mr Grant.'

'What man?'

'The man I told you about. The leader of the Western Somalia Liberation Front.'

'Where is he?'

'He's with the camelmen.'

'What's his name?'

'We call him Haji.'

And that was about the Arab equivalent of Smith. It was a title not a name and it just meant that he'd made the *hajj* to Mecca.

'OK. Bring him over.'

I saw an odd look on Aliki's face and I realized what I'd done. I stood up, brushing the sand from my clothes.

'Where does he want to talk?'

Issa smiled. 'He'll come over to you, Mr Grant. It's more private here.'

I stayed, standing, and when I half turned to look at Aliki she smiled and said softly, 'Good boy.' And I knew all too well what she meant. The condescending assumption that the man would come to me must have seemed typical British arrogance. And it was.

The man who came into the circle of light with Issa was

111

younger than me. He looked about thirty-five but I guessed he was nearer forty.

He stood looking at me for several moments, his eyes on my face as if he wanted to memorize my features. Then he smiled and held out his hand.

'You don't remember me?'

His voice was soft and his English was perfect. I took his hand.

'I apologize but I don't.'

He smiled and put his hand out palm downwards just above his knee.

'I was about so high when last we met.' He paused. Obviously amused at my not remembering him. And then he smiled as he said softly, 'Then again Abraham took a wife, and her name was Keturah. And she bore him Zimvan and Jokshan. And Jokshan begat Sheba, and Dedan. And the sons of Dedan were Asshurim and Letushim and Lenmim . . . and these are the days of Abraham's life which he lived, an hundred three score and fifteen years . . .'

And I could see him again in the light from my campfire all those years ago. His father watching intently as his small son did his duty for an honoured guest. Detailing his family lineage from Abraham. Telling his way through the years, decades and centuries until finally Yussuf Farrah begat Abdi Farah and his history lesson was up-to-date.

He laughed softly as recognition and surprise were obvious on my face and he said, 'You couldn't possibly have recognized me but I am pleased that you obviously remember me.'

'Is your father here too?'

'No. He was killed by the Ethiopians five, six years ago.'

'I'm sorry to hear that. He was an extraordinary man.'

He smiled. 'He was. I'm glad that you think that.'

'Sit down and join us. Can I introduce you to Aliki Yassou.'

He took her hand, kissed it politely and sat down with Issa, facing us. He wasted no time.

112

'I've come to ask your help. Even the help of the British government.'

'Before we talk about that tell me about you. Where did you learn this perfect English?'

He laughed. 'Three years at Magdalen and two years at the London School of Economics. That breeding home for wild revolutionaries who learn all they can from you and then go away and make a nuisance of themselves. Biting the hand that fed them.'

'And now?'

He shrugged. 'And now I try to reverse the injustice the British and Italians did to us when they gave our land to the Ethiopians.'

'You mean the Ogaden?'

'I mean the Ogaden.'

'I never understood why it was given to the Ethiopians. The only people in the Ogaden were Somalis.'

Haji smiled. 'It was a gift. A bribe. The West was worried about Russian and Chinese influence in Africa. The Emperor was pro-West. The Ogaden was there, in the gift of the United Nations. The Ethiopians had always wanted it but they had no possible legal claim to it. They never expected to get it. The world had never heard of the Ogaden. The British could have stopped it but they chose not to. On the 23rd September 1948 they handed out £91,000 to the Somali tribal headmen to settle all claims from the time of British rule and handed us over to the men in Addis Ababa. By the end of that day they were already killing Somalis. They killed twenty-five here in Jigjiga in the hour before sunset.'

'So why do you think the British might help you?'

He sighed. 'Mainly because they owe us that help but with the morals of the West we realize that that is a vain hope. But they may have learned a lesson. They must have or you would not be here. The Ethiopians have opened the doors for the Russians. Not just to Ethiopia but to the whole of East Africa. The West has no friends here but they have potential allies. My people are the only

113

ones who are capable of doing anything. Capable of helping.'

'Have you had any indication that London are willing to help you?'

He smiled. 'There are Americans and British in Mogadishu at this moment. Having what are referred to as "diplomatic discussions". They talk a lot and they promise a little. So far they have done nothing. We don't trust them but it is worth going along with their games in case there is something we can squeeze out of them.'

'Like what?'

'Weapons, guerrilla advisers, money, support in the UN or the Court of Human Rights. We ask for much and expect nothing. But trying costs us nothing but a small amount of pride.'

'Tell me how I can help.'

'That depends on why you are here.'

'I just want to identify where the Russians are stocking their weapons and supplies.'

'We can take you there. Nothing more than that?'

'Nothing that I can promise.'

'Where do you want to go?'

'Once I leave Jigjiga in any direction except back to Harar, I won't be able to go back to Addis. And the officials here will notify Addis the moment they see me leave.'

Haji smiled. 'Issa hired the Land-Rover in Harar and it's down here in Jigjiga. In one of the caves. You can drive it into the town, Issa will bring you back here in his car and we will take you on a detour in the night up to the Somali border. You can base yourself in Hargeisha. As soon as you wish we will take you to see the arms dump.'

'When do you want to do this?'

'Tomorrow night if you agree. There will be a good moon to help you drive in the dark.'

'How far is the detour?'

'About eighty kilometres.'

I looked at Aliki and she looked back at me. 'This is it,

sweetie. There's no going back once we've left here in the wrong direction. What do you think?'

She half smiled and said softly, 'for me it would not be the wrong direction.'

I turned to Haji. 'OK, Haji. Tomorrow night.'

He nodded. 'I'd like to speak to you alone for a few minutes.'

'There's nothing Aliki can't hear.'

But Aliki was already standing. 'I'll wait for you, Johnny. Don't be too long.'

I smiled. You'd have thought we were in a Wimbledon semi and I was going round to the local. Issa waved vaguely as he walked back towards the camelmen's fire. Haji took my hand and we walked towards the shadow of a termite hill. As we sat down he turned to look at me. 'We'll take care of Aliki for you if you want.'

'I think she'd prefer to stay on as part of the team.'

'What do you want to do when you've seen the arms dump?'

'I'll contact London and see what sort of response I get.'

'We're desperate for help, Johnny. The Ethiopians, helped by the Russians, are determined to wipe us out. And when they send the Cubans in and use the weapons in that dump we'll be finished. They'll kill us. Every one of us. Men, women and children.'

'What do you want London to do?'

'Destroy the dump. Give us a breathing space to get help from the Americans.'

'They won't send troops here, Haji.'

'I know. We ask them only for modern weapons and rockets. Missiles. Advisers.'

'They didn't like your people holding hands with the Russians.'

'We kicked them out.'

'Only when they had already started helping the Ethiopians.'

Haji shrugged. 'Today is today.'

'How many guerrillas have you got?'

115

'Five thousand. More if I need them.'

'Let's talk again when I've seen the dump and contacted London.'

'How long do you intend staying in the Ogaden?'

'A few days. A week at the most. I've got a business in London. I've been away too long already.'

'We'd better go back to Aliki. I'll take you to the other Land-Rover in the morning and we'll put yours under the cliff.'

As we stood by the Land-Rover Haji said, 'Thank you for anything you can do for us.' Then he turned to walk away and said softly, '*Salaam aleikum*.' I said it back to him.

It seemed a long time before I slept after we had made love. Maybe it was making love that did it. Maybe it was just events catching up with me but I suddenly felt that I didn't belong in all this. It was crazy. I was a photographer. I'd got a successful business that I was neglecting. I hadn't even told them how long I should be away. I could have been between those cool silk sheets in my Chelsea flat, not lying cramped in the back of a Land-Rover in Africa. I'd met plenty of men during the war who liked playing Lawrence of Arabia but I wasn't one of them. I had a natural inclination to the fleshpots of London. Or Paris or Rome. Why the hell should I get mixed up again with African politics, and the feuding between Amharas and Somalis? They all nurtured their tribal rivalries. Killing and hating each other for the sake of some long gone insult or cattle raid. The Somalis were as warlike with one another as with the Ethiopians and Kenyans. They may be beautiful and elegant but they were just as savage as the rest of them. My Aliki wasn't really a Somali. She might look like one but Kathi Yassou was all Greek.

I dreamed that night that it was snowing. I could hear hailstones on the canvas roof of the Land- Rover.

It was Issa rapping on the tailboard that eventually woke me. For once he was smiling. It was nearly ten and the white man was probably exhausted from having his woman too many times. When I pulled back the flaps properly I saw why he was smiling. Thick clouds of locusts were swirling and wheeling as far as the eye could see. The hailstones from my dream.

Issa shrugged. 'They will help us. You could leave as soon as you're back here. Maybe two hours' time. They won't be watching us with this. It stretches for miles, probably back to the Red Sea.'

The fantastic swarms of hoppers and full-grown locusts had always been bad in this area but I'd never seen a swarm like this. The sound of their brittle wings was everywhere and the sun was hazy behind the shimmering clouds of insects.

I left Aliki to pack our things and went with Issa to the overhang in the rock-face where he had left the other Land-Rover and he followed me in his car as I drove to Jigjiga. I left the Land-Rover not far from the army commander's shack and walked to the coffee-shop to meet Issa. The town had battened down the hatches against the locusts. The shops were closed and the stalls empty. The crisp, dry bodies of locusts snapped and crackled underfoot as I walked across to the coffee-shop. It was closed but Issa was there, in his car. A cloud of locusts came in with me as I opened the door and slid into the passenger seat. I spent the next twenty minutes as we drove back to the mountains swatting locusts from the inside of the windscreen, and on the outside the windscreen-wipers worked constantly to scrape the debris of *kamikaze* locusts until the build-up of crushed bodies almost stopped the wipers from moving at all.

I checked the Land-Rover for petrol, oil and water then Haji and Aliki squashed into the front seat with me and we set off.

For half an hour I followed Haji's directions across the sand from one termite hill to another, down into long dried-up *wadis*, and half an hour later the heat really hit us as we came clear of the locust swarm into the full heat of the midday sun. I stopped the vehicle and got out to check the tyres. They were as hard as rock but the covers seemed to be holding. Driving across hard sand in these temperatures plays havoc with tyres. The constant pounding and the burning heat of the sand build up the internal pressures and if you don't bleed them the covers slowly disintegrate into long strands of shredded rubber that flay the inner canvas to destruction. In the old days the RAF had to drop me a set of new tyres every eight days. As I pressed the valves one after the other the stench of the hot air from inside the suffering tyres was nauseating.

Haji stood with me as I looked around through the binoculars. The desert was giving way to patches of low scrub. Thorn bushes and a kind of pygmy cactus. But as far as the shimmering horizon there was no sign of life or feature on the terrain.

Several times we crossed tracks but Haji ignored them and we were taking a long curving route that was leaving the sun behind us. It was mid-afternoon when we came to a *wadi*, its dank, rotting odour overlaying even our petrol fumes. But I knew that *wadi*. I'd passed across it dozens of times in the old days and it meant that we were already over the frontier. We were in Somalia, about twenty kilometres from Hargeisha.

We camped about two kilometres from the outskirts of the town and as we sat around the fire later it was Aliki who got to the point.

'When can we go to see the dump, Haji?'

He shrugged. 'Tomorrow. It's up to Johnny.' He looked at me, eyebrows raised.

'Have you got men who've seen it already who could describe it?'

'Yes. I can have them here by tomorrow. I'll go into Hargeisha tonight and bring them back in the morning.'

'Let's do that.'

Ten minutes later Haji turned and waved as he headed away from our camp towards the town. A tall, lean figure in his Somali robe of small red and white squares of gingham that wouldn't have looked out of place on a girl at a vicarage garden party. It was strange enough for me to be back in Somalia but for Haji it must be even more complex. What good was a degree in philosophy in the Ogaden desert? What strange loyalty would drive a man back to this arid piece of the earth's surface and its handsome nomads? Somalis aren't Africans despite living in Africa. They don't seek a settled life or even an improvement in their conditions. They despise men who own and care for cattle, and no Somali would demean himself and his tribe by cultivating land. Their wealth is camels, and all they ask of God and man is to be left alone to follow the sparse rains as they have done since the days before Muhammad. Intensely proud, and almost unbearably arrogant, they tolerate as equals the foreigners who rule them from time to time and despise all others. Openly and provocatively.

I looked across at Aliki and she said, 'Why did you smile when we came to the *wadi* today?'

'You're very observant, my love. It reminded me of something that happened when I was in Hargeisha in the old days. It wasn't funny at the time, though.'

'Tell me.'

'We set up a radio station in tents. For the troops. It was to provide entertainment and news for the brigades stationed around here and Borama. Three or four hours every evening with fifteen minutes in Somali. The day before we started I had a deputation of tribal leaders. Sheikhs and *khadis*. The rains were ten days late. Could they broadcast prayers for rain, to start off the first day's programmes? I thought it was a great idea. Pleasing the locals and good propaganda. They said their prayers starting at six o'clock the next night. An hour later the rains broke. It was the big rains. Everybody was impressed and delighted. At three in the morning the radio station had been swept away on the flood from the *wadi* we crossed. Everything ended up miles away.

119

Transmitters, tents, even a piano, ended up in down-stream thorn trees. You can guess who got the blame.'

She smiled and then leaned forward and kissed me gently. 'I wish I'd known you in those days.'

'Why?'

She shrugged, still smiling. 'In those days you didn't have to worry about us Somalis. You just got on with your war. And even that was different from all this. No missiles and satellites. No Russians, no Cubans.'

'Don't worry, honey. We'll get by. Do our good deed for Haji and Shapiro and then bow out gracefully. Back to London and civilization.'

'Tell me about civilization.'

It sounded such an innocent, childlike question, but it wasn't. And I knew from her eyes and the faint, amused smile that it wasn't meant to be simple.

'Theatres, art galleries, concerts, books, comfort, discussion, discrimination and taste.' I smiled. 'That's the best I can do.'

'And diplomats who are professional liars and deceivers. Indifference to tens of thousands of other people dying of starvation. Exploitation of small countries because of their natural resources, their cheap labour and their usefulness as a military base. Every man for himself and against all others. For money and power. Civilization?'

There were answers to most of those points but I wasn't in the mood to give them.

'Let's go to bed, honey. At least that's much the same all over the world.'

She smiled and stood up. And just the way she stood up was beautiful. All Somali girls moved as if they'd had at least four years at the Royal Ballet. And when they walked it was a wonder to behold. Long legs moving from the hips not the knees, aware of their grace and attraction but with a smile that dismissed all men for what they were. Lecherous small boys who knew more about camels than women.

120

12

Haji came for us just after nine and we drove back with
him into the town. Hargeisha had always been called a
town even when it had only half a dozen permanent
buildings, but it really was a town now. I parked the
Land-Rover in the square and we walked with Haji to a
coffee-shop. Through bead curtains, down a small pas-
sage to a room with a table and several chairs. There
were three Somalis standing, waiting for us.

We talked for nearly three hours, Haji and Aliki
interpreting for me. I drew diagrams, squares and rec-
tangles, extending and reducing as they gave their descriptions. Even allowing for ignorance and exaggerations
it sounded an incredible installation. If the landing-
strip dimensions they had given were anywhere near
accurate it was a landing-strip for jets. If they were
correct there were at least thirty store blocks. Some
under camouflaged canvas and some housed in factory-
built wood and asbestos sheds assembled on site. The
whole complex was sited about twenty kilometres inside
the Ethiopian border. It was an odd place to have a
weapons dump unless it was to be used against the
Somalis.

Two of them had watched the big choppers bringing in
the stores, and from what they described there were
tanks and tracked vehicles and hundreds of large crates.

By early evening I had worked out a rough-and-ready
reconnaissance plan. It was more a reconnaissance for a
reconnaissance, for I knew far too little to risk anything
complicated. It was just a look at the target.

121

The three Somalis were ready to go with us but I insisted that Aliki stayed in Hargeisha.

Haji and Aliki were amused that evening as I tried on the Somali robe that Haji had brought for me, but by the time Aliki had gone over me with the juice of some nuts I looked a reasonable counterfeit of a camelman.

We started off just after dark. Aliki drove us as far as the *wadi* and we kept alongside its banks for the first couple of hours. Despite the moonlight it was slow going and I estimated that at the end of the first hour we had done no more than five or six kilometres. The rough leather sandals I had to wear didn't help. I didn't have those thick hard calloused soles to my feet that Haji and the others had accumulated long ago when they were kids.

Then, quite noticeably, the *wadi* swung west and two hours later we were facing a gentle slope and Haji stopped. Two of the men went down and crawled to the ridge of the slope. They were out of sight now and we sat in silence waiting for them to return. It was ten minutes before one of them came back, kneeling in the sand as he whispered to Haji. Haji looked at me for a moment and then turned to nod at the third man who crawled away into the darkness.

Five minutes later I thought I heard a sound in the darkness but it was another ten minutes before the three men came stumbling down the slope. As they got near I saw that one was carrying a rifle. An old-fashioned Lee Enfield. And the others were dragging something behind them.

The something was the corpse of an Ethiopian. He had been a perimeter lookout and Haji went through his clothes and took his pay-book and documents. The Somalis said he had only just taken over from the old watch and that should give us four hours before they discovered that he was missing. Apparently officers never carried out checks on perimeter guards while they were on duty. The Somalis stripped off his clothes and folded them carefully before they buried them in the sand. Until they picked up

122

the naked body and the head rolled back I hadn't noticed that the throat had been sliced through. I told Haji to stay with the others until I came back and I crawled to the top of the ridge.

It was all much nearer than I had imagined and it was like a stage set. I'd expected just the light of the moon but the whole complex behind the barbed wire was lit by spotlights on towers like a POW camp. There was a faint hum of generators and that was all. It was as silent as the rest of the desert and no sign of guards or patrols. If they had just silenced the Ethiopian we could have taken him back and interrogated him. It was ridiculous to have killed a man who could have told us so much. As I swept the glasses from one end of the site to the other the details they had given me seemed to be reasonably accurate but there was nothing more we could do that night.

The early ground wind was already driving the top layer of sand across the surface of the desert as I crawled back to Haji. I told him to order his men to drag the corpse as far as they could go towards the camp without being seen. I didn't want whoever was in charge of the guard to know exactly where he had been killed. They were away for twenty minutes. Haji seemed very angry but it wasn't the time to talk, not even in whispers. It would have to wait until we got back. He would know that his men should have taken the man prisoner for interrogation.

It was the false dawn by the time we got to the *wadi* and I was relieved when I saw the lights of the Land-Rover flash briefly as we got to the top of the bank.

Haji had found us a small wooden villa to stay in and I decided that we'd better make a rough plan without any more waiting. I contacted London with a brief two-sentence message about the location of the arms dump and a rough guess at its map reference. They acknowledged, asked me to wait and then indicated that there was no further traffic and I stood down. Vaguely irritated by everybody.

There was only one obvious thing to do and that was to

go back that night and get another guard and interrogate him about the layout and the security precautions. Haji agreed, but it meant going to a different spot on the perimeter to make sure that we weren't expected after they found the guard's body. Haji said that he and his men would rather go alone. It made sense. They moved far quicker on their own and they knew the terrain as well as I knew the King's Road, Chelsea.

He was in his thirties, an Amhara from just south of Addis. He'd been in the army four years. And he was scared of what we were going to do to him.

Aliki was the only one who spoke Amharic well enough to talk to him. There were three Russians and a dozen Cubans in charge of the dump. He didn't know the names of any of them, just giving vague physical descriptions to identify them. They were all referred to as colonels although none of them wore uniforms. Apparently there were constant rows between them but the Cubans always ended doing what the Russians wanted. But best of all was the description of the security arrangements. If the man's description was anywhere near accurate the security was primitive indeed. They had mined the outer area in the first few weeks but so many guards had been killed that all the mines had been removed. Only six men covered a perimeter that was over three miles long. A barbed-wire perimeter and a two-man walking patrol were the only other precautions apart from infrequent random inspections by the Cubans or the Russians. It was interesting to learn that the tensions between the two groups were enough to have made them set up separate administrative and living quarters. The Ethiopians saw the Russians as efficient but grim. They disliked the Cubans because over a dozen young girls had been shipped down from Harar for the Cubans' entertainment. Ethiopians had not been allowed to bring wives or girlfriends, and no female company had been provided for them by the *derg*.

The Ethiopian had too little knowledge of sophisticated weapons to be able to identify much of what was in the dump but from his description there were vast numbers of light tanks and tracked vehicles and what sounded like both mobile and static missile launchers. What was surprising was the numbers of helicopters he described. Troop transporters and at least two other types that I couldn't identify.

I decided that I'd contact London before I made any more moves. London responded immediately as I tapped out the longest message that I'd sent them so far. They acknowledged and asked me to come back on net in thirty minutes. Thirty minutes later they came back. I was to wait and make no attempt to go in myself until I'd had further instructions. They gave me a list of times to contact them for the next forty-eight hours.

I gave Haji the news and one of his contacts sent a messenger for him an hour later, leaving Aliki and me alone.

The shack we were in was like the setting of one of those Somerset Maugham stories in Malaya. Cane chairs and cane table. An old-fashioned bed with brass finials, a faded photograph of King George VI on one wall, and a portable gramophone on a coffee-table in the far corner. A dozen tattered paperbacks on a shelf, with a clock whose once-white face was now pockmarked with rust spots, and a moth-eaten umbrella propped in a sugar basin in one corner, its cover green and iridescent with age. And to round things off a ceiling fan with blades that looked big enough for a small helicopter.

Aliki and I walked around the township and the changes were incredible. Small shops, wooden houses, even some houses built of clay blocks, a car repair shop, a tannery, a silversmith and a couple of bakers in just the area we strolled through. We had a coffee in a *duka* and then it was time to head back to the shack. The message when it came through from London was to wait, with no radio contacts necessary until the following day. Somebody had put a box of foodstuffs on the small table and

Aliki was sorting them out when I went back into the shack carrying the radio with me.

'D'you think I should get one of Haji's men to guard the Land-Rover?'

She smiled. 'You don't trust us Somalis?'

I shrugged. 'Well, it has been known for things to go missing.'

She was laughing, hands on hips. Somalis were the most consummate thieves in the whole world. I had once left my car unguarded for barely twenty minutes in Mogadishu and when I went to drive off, the engine started OK but nothing else happened when I let in the clutch. They had taken off all the wheels, propping the axles up neatly with wooden blocks. A wheel could fetch over a hundred pounds even in those days' money. Soldiers sleeping in camp-beds with British sentries properly mounted had lost not only their rifles but the clothes and boots they were actually wearing at the time, without being aware of their sleep being disturbed for even a moment. Somalis did it with real style. When Aliki stopped laughing she said, 'They won't do it to you, Johnny. Haji will have put the word around.'

'I hope he's careful about what he tells them.'

The smile faded and she said softly, 'Tell me what's the matter, Johnny. You're all tensed up. Wanting to explode.'

'I'm not. I just don't want other people to make this thing more unsafe than it already is.'

'Are you regretting being involved in all this?'

It was a question I didn't want to answer. The answer that would please her would be a lie, and the real answer would not only disappoint her but might even affect our relationship. I knew I'd rather lie than do that but I didn't want to lie. In the few seconds of these thoughts she reached across the table and covered my hand with hers.

'You don't have to answer that, Johnny. It was an unfair question.'

'There isn't a straightforward answer, honey. I resent

126

Joe Shapiro getting me involved, but now I am involved I mean to help your people if I can.'

'Why?'

'Because I love you.'

'Nothing else?'

'You mean I should help them because they deserve to be helped?'

She nodded. 'Yes.'

'They do deserve to be helped but I don't exactly go along with the idea that it should be me who does it.'

'So why don't we just say so and go back to Mogadishu and catch a plane to Europe?' She shrugged. 'You're absolutely right. It isn't your responsibility. It isn't anything to do with you. It's just an accident that you were here in the war. Let's tell them all to go to hell.'

I smiled and some of the tension drained away. 'We'll do what we said we'd do, and then call it a day. There's something else I ought to tell you.'

'What's that?' And I saw the concern on her face. It wasn't fair.

'I love you, Aliki Yassou, for all the days of my life plus one.'

The big eyes closed with relief but she laughed softly. 'You'd better bring in the lamp from the car, it's getting dark.'

Despite the rough-and-ready mosquito net on the windows and the closed door, the pressure lamp had attracted the usual squadrons of insects flinging themselves against it and expiring noisily on the floor and the table. In the end I put out the lamp and lit a candle. Its soft light made Aliki look even more beautiful. I could see the flame reflected in her big brown eyes.

'Can I ask you a silly question?' she said.

'Ask away.'

'Why did you ask me to marry you so soon after we met?'

'Because I loved you as soon as I saw you.'

127

She smiled. 'You mean you wanted to sleep with me as soon as you saw me?'

'It was more than that. But that was part of it.'

'How could you love me when you knew nothing about me?'

'Just instinct.'

'What did you love about me?'

'You're terribly beautiful but you don't take it seriously. You don't draw attention to it. And you seemed to be a very proud person, and independent. You had no independence in fact. You were entirely dependent on other people.' I smiled. 'I felt you needed to be looked after.'

'A lame duck, or maybe a lame swan?'

'Not lame. Caged, but not lame.'

'Why didn't you ever marry?'

I shrugged. 'I did marry. Right after the end of the war. It lasted six months. Nobody's fault. Just the wrong people for one another. We got divorced and it was a terrible relief. Like being let out of prison. Or waking up from a bad dream.'

'But you had girlfriends.'

'Yes. Of course.'

'And you slept with them? Had sex with them?'

'Yes.'

'But you didn't love them?'

'I liked them. One or two I cared about but it wasn't more than that.'

'And now that you've known me longer?'

'You mean how do I feel?'

'Yes.'

'Nothing's changed. I just love you. I always will. I don't need to keep digging up the rose bush and checking the roots to see how it's doing.'

'But you know more about me now.'

'That makes no difference. It just . . . I don't know how to explain it . . .' I shrugged and smiled. 'Knowing you longer just makes it more solid.'

'And my life before you. The Russians in Addis. What about all that?'

'You mean am I jealous about them?'

'Yes.'

'Yes, I'm jealous about them. And angry. But that will fade in time.'

'Why angry?'

'Angry that it was what it was. No caring. No love.'

'You're a strange man.'

'In what way?'

'I remember what you did to Panov that night at the Hilton in Addis. That's you. Very tough and very sure of yourself. Not at all afraid. And just now you were angry that those men didn't care about me.' She smiled. 'You're a romantic . . . but a very tough romantic. That's why *I* said "yes" so quickly.'

'I'm glad you did.'

I wasn't due to go on net to London until noon, local time, and I drove us out a few miles on the Berbera road. Berbera had been a small fishing port and the starting-point for small dhows taking pilgrims to Mecca, but it was a real port now, with deep-water facilities, thanks to the Russians in their clumsy and brief courtship of the Somalis.

In the old days there was no road, just a track in the sand. In fact there had been only fifty kilometres of road in the whole of Somalia, the road built by the Italians from Mogadishu to Bulo Burti where the good metalled road suddenly ended and became just one more track through the sand and termite hills.

But the Berbera road now was obviously passable even in the rains and that was real progress. I stopped about twelve kilometres outside Hargeisha and we got out for a stretch and a coffee from the Thermos. There were a few tufts of tussocky grass, a sprinkling of camelthorn and bushes that looked like gorse.

Aliki pointed. 'What kind of birds are those, Johnny?'

There was a flock of five or six black and white birds fluttering tentatively in the camelthorn. I'd never known their proper names. Like most unidentifiable birds we knew them in the old days as 'shite-hawks' but that wasn't for my lady.

'They're some kind of guinea fowl. Tough as iron even if you boil them all night.'

And as I spoke a small plane circled in the distance towards Hargeisha. It looked like a Cessna but against the glare of the sun I couldn't be sure. It looked as if it was coming in to land.

We had our coffee and sat at the side of the track for ten minutes or so and then climbed back into the Land-Rover. I had to soak towels in water from the jerry-cans before we could sit on the canvas seats. And I needed wet cloths before I could hold the steering-wheel. You could literally have fried an egg anywhere on the vehicle.

Haji was waiting for us at our shack and when we were inside he took a small package from inside his robe, holding it out to me.

'What is it, Haji?'

'I've no idea. Maybe you should look inside.'

I opened it carefully. It was a small Olympus camera. It was a very small 35mm XA2. There were four rolls of Kodak Tri-X black and white film in their original cartons. No note. No indication of why I'd got it. I looked at Haji.

'Who gave it to you?'

'It came by light plane from Mogadishu about twenty minutes ago. It was delivered to the provincial governor with instructions to hand it over to you. That's all I know.'

'But who sent it?'

'I don't know. But it must have been someone high up to be able to send a plane and to be able to give orders to the governor.'

'The governor must know who gave him the orders.'

'Of course. But he wouldn't tell me and he won't tell you.'

I put the camera on the table and looked at my watch.

130

The mystery would have to stay unsolved. I was due on air to London in fifteen minutes.

I backed the Land-Rover into the shade at the side of the shack and put up the long thin aerial and plugged in the Morse key and the headphones. I took the long leads to the spare battery and switched on. Exactly on the hour London came up. The message was short and precise. And solved the mystery of the camera at the same time. They wanted photographs from inside the dump. As many as possible. And as soon as possible. When it was done I should notify the local governor and a plane would be sent for Aliki and me to take us to Mogadishu. They asked for an acknowledgement and an indication of how long I would need. I gave them the acknowledgement and ignored the question.

Back inside I told Aliki and Haji what London wanted. I got the impression that Haji already knew.

'We'll have to do it quickly, Johnny. The small rains start in four days' time. The *wadi* will be in flood. It's impassable after the first few hours.'

They were called the small rains because they only lasted about ten days, but while they were on the rain came lashing down to crashes of thunder with tropical violence. It was actually painful in its ferocity. Even the wandering Somali herdsmen huddled under their goatskin tents until the rains ended.

13

There was a distant flash of lightning as we got to the ridge, then another that lit up the arms dump as if it was a theatre set, but there was no thunder. We were about ten yards short of the barbed wire when the first clap of thunder burst overhead, the sky bright with simultaneous flashes of lightning. Then silence, as if the world was waiting. The next explosion of thunder coincided with the lightning and the air was suddenly cold. It looked as if the rains were coming early.

I clipped carefully through the strands of wire and bent them back to let Haji and the other man through. The other man was wearing the dead Ethiopian's uniform. None of us spoke Amharic, Spanish or Russian but the coming storm seemed to have cleared the whole area. I prayed that the lights would stay on. Without them there was no chance of taking photographs. It was available light or nothing.

The first store was a large long tent like an army EPIP. The flaps were already open, probably to try and keep down the temperature. There were long lines of wheeled howitzers and hundreds of small missiles stacked upwards, their bases in wooden racks, but there was no time to try and identify what they were. I just kept the camera clicking. In the next tent were scores of tracked vehicles and pyramids of shells.

The disguised Somali led the way and Haji acted as arse-end Charlie watching my rear. When we got to the wooden buildings it was just crates. Some huge ones and some that were long and narrow. As I went into the third wooden building I heard a gasp and at the far end I saw the Somali with his hand over a white man's throat, his long knife thrusting deep into the man's back, again and again.

More crates and a long line of tank engines mounted in wooden frames and then it came. A clap of thunder, lightning that illuminated the inside of the tent and the first drops of rain. It sounded like heavy hailstones but it wasn't, it was the first flurry of rain. When the real rain started the noise would be deafening.

Haji shouted in my ear, 'We must go, Johnny. The rain will be already an hour ahead of us from the hills.'

Nobody tried to stop us as we made our way back to the gap in the wire. I'd taken one whole cassette. Thirty-six exposures and I was sure that wouldn't be enough. But it was all I could do.

It took us an hour to get to the *wadi* and it had been too long. It was still not raining there but the rains had broken way over in the hills. They were thirty kilometres away but as they gathered the torrential rain they spewed a flood of water to the three big *wadis* that fanned out down the flattened contours. The water was already swirling past, shoving the accumulated debris of months ahead of it like a bulldozer shovelling earth. Tree-trunks, excrement, piles of thorn bushes and the swollen corpses of goats and sheep.

Aliki briefly flashed the lights of the Land-Rover but there seemed little chance of her seeing the flash from my torch. There was no moon now. Just black skies and the roar of the river as it headed towards Dikeleh.

It would take an hour for the debris to clear but in that hour the water would be within a couple of feet of the top of the *wadi's* banks. A few hours later the banks would burst under the strain and the flood would spread for miles on each side of the newly-born river.

Neither Haji nor the Somali could swim. Somalis seldom could. Unless they lived on the coast they had no chance to learn. And the coast was for sailors and fishermen. The land near the coast was too brackish even for animals.

It was then I heard the Land-Rover start and I could just see its headlights as it disappeared into the darkness. She was going to get help but I doubted if there was any help that Hargeisha could provide. Then from the direction of the dump I heard the clatter of a chopper. I could see its belly-light as it headed towards the *wadi* about a mile upstream. I shouted to Haji and his man to get covered in the sand, heads down. They'd probably found the dead Cuban or Russian, whatever he was. Killing Ethiopians didn't matter but killing white men called for action.

The chopper was weaving from side to side of the *wadi*, its light illuminating a circle of almost a hundred yards, and from time to time the gunner fired off a dozen or so rounds. Aimlessly but dangerously. I pressed my face into the sand as it swept over us sucking up clouds of sand that must have precluded any visibility at ground level from the chopper's cabin. Then it swung off in a wide circle and headed back towards the dump.

The three of us sat there waiting. But what we were expecting we had no idea. We were right on the edge of the rain cloud and we could hear it pounding the sand about a hundred yards away. The curtain of water crept slowly towards us. Half an hour later it hit us. It was icy cold, taking my breath away, leaving me gasping as I bent over to take it on my back. None of us heard the vehicles come back to the far side of the *wadi* but when I lifted my head for a moment I saw the lights. There were at least two other vehicles beside the Land-Rover, silhouetted in each other's headlights. Then the white lights went out, but I could see the faint fuzz of hand-held lamps moving about. Then suddenly a headlight was flashing and it was in Morse. SOS twice and then w – a – i – t. I crawled over to the others and told them what the lights had said. They were both shivering violently and their faces were almost white. I stayed with them, watching and waiting.

Ten minutes later the lights flashed again. Slowly, letter

by letter. FIRINGROPESHINETORCH. It didn't dawn on me for several seconds what it meant and then I told Haji and his man to get ready to grab the rope as it came over. Then the headlights flickered ONEMINUTE.

I heard the crack of the charge and then the rope snaked over our heads. We clawed frantically for it until it was swept away by the force of the river. It had been right on target and not one of us had even touched it. I placed us in a rough triangle, with me at the apex at the rear. I was too blinded by the rain and too far back to read the next flicker of lights but this time when the rope came snaking over it was slower and I got it. They had weighted it with a small grab anchor and I had to lean back to stop the pressure of the water against the rope in the river from forcing me into the *wadi*.

I made Haji go first so that his man could watch what to do. Somalis are not physically strong but they are sinewy with tremendous stamina. I saw Haji's head disappear into the foaming brown water and then the car lights were casting shadows and I lost sight of him. It seemed like hours before the lights flashed again but it was only ten minutes. When the Somali went in he screamed as he felt the force of the water but he held on. Then he was out of sight. It was fifteen minutes before they signalled again.

The rope was nylon, about an inch and a half thick. The kind of rope that was used on pleasure boats. I circled it twice round my waist, knotted it, and held my breath as I slithered clumsily into the water. For long frightening moments I felt as if I were flying as the mass of heavy water carried me downstream. With nobody holding my end of the rope I could only heave myself inch by inch along the rope. But there was nothing I could do until it was taut. I struggled to try and get my head above water and then suddenly the rope was tight in my hands. The rush of water was sweeping me in an arc towards the other bank and I wondered if it might sweep me to safety more speedily than me hauling on the rope. Then there was a blinding pain in my chest and the last thing I could

135

remember was my hands loosing the rope and my body turning slowly like in a dream.

I could see Joe Shapiro's face reflected in the clear water, its reflection shimmering then breaking up as the water rippled smoothly, and there were voices far away. And then the light from the water was too much and I closed my eyes.

It was two days later when I came to again. Aliki was there and it wasn't water I could see but reflections on the white ceiling of the hospital room. And there was a Somali girl in nurse's uniform. Aliki bent over and kissed my mouth and said, 'Welcome back, Johnny.'

'What's going on?' And my voice sounded slurred and a long way away.

'You hurt your chest. You were hit by a tree in the *wadi*.'

'Where am I?'

'You're in the hospital in Mogadishu.'

'How in hell did I get here?'

'They brought us by plane. They were very worried about you.'

'How long have I been here?'

'Just over two days.'

I went to sit up and somebody seemed to hit my chest with a hammer.

'Don't move, Johnny. You broke two ribs and they're all bound up in plaster.'

The sweat poured down my face and I said, 'I dreamed about Shapiro. Have you heard from him at all?'

'He's here. Waiting to talk with you when you're better.'

'What happened to the camera and the films?'

She smiled. 'They're OK. The camera was still hung around your neck. Joe said the photographs were fine.'

'Where is he?'

'He's at the consulate. I've got a suite at the hotel.'

'The Croce del Sud?'

136

She smiled. 'Yes.'

'My God. I hope it's better than it used to be.'

'It's fine, Johnny. Don't worry about anything.'

'How did they get me out?'

She smiled. 'They hauled you in on the end of the rope like a great big shark.'

'Where did they get the rockets for the rope?'

'They got hold of the captain of the governor's official boat. A Somali who'd been in the Royal Navy. Your navy. He was great.' She leaned over and looked at my face. 'I was so worried about you.' She kissed me gently. 'Get some sleep and I'll be here tomorrow when you wake up.'

14

I'd always liked Mogadishu. It was a lively town, almost entirely Italian in appearance and the Somalis and Italians had always got on quite well together. Not politically, but in day-to-day living. The Somalis valued the Italians' skills, and loved the money pouring in, and the Italian expatriates from the poor south of Italy valued their farmsteads and loved the pretty Somali girls. When the British army threw the Italians out a lot of the life went out of Mogadishu but it had had enough personality to survive the military government and retain some of its former gaiety.

There were more buildings now, and very few Italians, but it could have been almost any small town on the seacoast of Calabria. A kind of flat Amalfi. The hotel, the Croce del Sud, was still the same. Old-fashioned but with ambitions to stateliness. It could have been a British Railways hotel for some town that had once seen better days.

As I looked around the suite I noticed that they had brought down all my wooden boxes. There was an envelope on the table. It was a note from Joe Shapiro and thirty-six postcard-sized photographs. It seemed a long time ago and I was glad that it was all over.

The note said:

Dear J.
You always were an awkward bastard. Looking forward to seeing you. Thanks for the pretty pictures. More important than we thought. Much more.
    See you.
                                    J.S.

I lay on the bed for an hour, pleased to be independent again, and happy to be alone with Aliki.

'I missed you, honey.'

She laughed. 'You didn't, you silly man, you were unconscious most of the time.'

'Thanks for the rescue operation.'

'The governor took personal charge. I just stood around waiting.'

'I can't believe that.'

'You might as well. I reverted to type and wailed like any Somali girl at a funeral.'

I patted the bed beside me and she walked over, smiling.

We took dinner in our room that night or I might have seen them sooner. The three of them were at a table on the patio when we went down for breakfast. Jonnet, Peers and his wife. Peers glaced at us and then looked away, pretending a great interest in his avocado. He was saying something to Jonnet who ostentatiously didn't turn to look at us.

We had almost finished our coffee and croissants when I saw Joe Shapiro crossing the wide dining-room, heading towards us. I shook my head as unobtrusively as I could and saw him turn away towards the main hall. He was at the far end of our corridor when we went back to our room. I left the door ajar and he came in a few moments later. All smiles and congratulations. London had been shocked by the photographs. There were to be high-level talks with the Somalis and I was to be there.

'I'll have Aliki with me, Joe. She's part of the team.'

'Sure. Sure.' But I could see the frustration on his face.

'What was London so shocked about?'

He shrugged. 'Practically all of it. Very little of it would be of any use fighting the Somali guerrillas in the Ogaden. Not even if the Somali army pitches in with them unofficially. Amphibious personnel carriers where there ain't any rivers. Antimissile missiles, ground-to-air missiles, air-to-air missiles. Against what? Not the Somalis. OK,

139

they'll chew them up first, but machine guns, a few howitzers and a spotter plane could see them off. Those Russkies in Addis are heading for Nairobi, that's for sure. And we ain't gonna let them get away with that.'

'But you'd let them wipe out the Somalis?'

Shapiro looked embarrassed. 'Of course not. If they ask us formally for help then they'll get it.'

'What kind of help?'

'Diplomatic, economic. All the pressures we can bring on Addis and Moscow.'

'But no arms. No military help?'

'That wouldn't be for me to decide. You know that.'

'Neither would the rest of it, but you said it could be done all the same.'

Joe smiled. His patient, diplomatic, dealing-with-idiots smile. 'Let's leave it until we talk with the government people here. You know this girl has had practically no sleep for two weeks.'

It was a cheap, patronizing cop-out, diverting attention from the realities at Aliki's expense. I ignored it and said, 'When do we talk with the government people?'

'We're waiting for you. This afternoon if you want.'

'Who'll be there?'

'I'm not sure. I'll be there anyway.' Joe Shapiro's bushy eyebrows went up as he looked across at me. 'Are you angry with me for some reason, Johnny?'

'I just want to get the hell out of here and back to London. I've done what you asked me to do. I can't contribute anything to any talks.'

Shapiro said nothing. Eyebrows still raised. And then he stood up. 'I'll leave you two in peace.' He paused. 'I'll be in touch, Johnny.'

When he had left us Aliki said, '*Are* you annoyed with Joe?'

'Yes.'

'Why?'

'I don't want to be involved in any talks. Let them sort it out themselves, whatever it may be.'

140

She smiled. 'We've got a lifetime, Johnny. A day or two won't hurt us.'

'Don't count on it, honey. I don't trust those bastards.'

'Which bastards?'

I waved my hands around, annoyed at not being able to say what I meant. Not because she wouldn't understand but because I didn't know myself what I meant.

'Any of them. Shapiro. London. Somali politicians. The whole bloody lot.'

She smiled. 'Time for your antibiotic.'

I walked with Aliki to the British consulate. It's always as well to sign the book when you're somewhere that's on the boil.

There was a Somali clerk at the reception desk and I told him that I wanted to sign the book and then see the consul. Just to say 'hello'. He smiled and took the visitors' book from the long drawer in his desk. It was already open and I borrowed his pen and signed my name and put in the date and gave the hotel as my address.

The clerk looked surprised when Aliki took the pen and he spoke quickly in Somali and she answered him.

'What did he say?'

'He wanted to see my passport.'

'Have you got it with you?'

'Yes.'

She reached into her handbag and as she took out the blue passport I took it from her and said, 'Just write your passport number in the last column and initial it.'

'He wants to see it.'

'Tell him to go to hell.'

'But he's an official clerk.'

'I know. Just do as I say.'

And she did. And I gave her back the passport. I turned to the clerk. 'Tell the consul I want to see him.'

'Yes, sir.'

When he had gone Aliki put her arm through mine and said, 'Don't get worked up, Johnny. He's only a clerk.

141

You know Somalis. They love a bit of bureaucratic power.'

It was ten minutes before the clerk came back and I waited impatiently. There was a photograph of the Queen on the wall and a separate one of Philip. There was a smaller photograph of a Somali wearing a military cap, its peak covered with braid. It was a flat face for a Somali. Black eyes staring, the uniform collar tight enough to make a fold in the flesh of his thick neck. I guessed it was their top man. Major General Muhammad Siad Barre. President of the Somali Democratic Republic. Not an elected president but victor of a coup.

And then the little man was back.

'Mr Rogers is not available at the moment, sir. He sends you his compliments and will contact you later at the hotel.'

'What's Mr Rogers doing?'

He shrugged. 'I don't know, sir. Working I am sure.'

I pointed at the door. 'Is that his office?'

He nodded but didn't speak. He lifted his arm tentatively to stop me as I headed for the closed door. As I opened it I saw a man sitting at a desk, pouring himself a whisky. He had sparse, wispy red hair and the pale skin and freckles that go with red hair. He looked up, surprised.

'I say,' he said, 'what's going on?'

'I wondered what you were doing that was more important than seeing two British nationals. You can't get that many British visitors in Mog. Have you got a drink problem, Rogers?'

He stood up slowly. 'You'd better get out of my office before I call one of the guards.'

'Call them, then.'

Like all bureaucrats he was quick at working out the odds. He half smiled, ingratiatingly, 'Look old chap. I'm only carrying out orders. No offence meant. We have to be at arm's length with you secret service chaps or we get heap big trouble.'

142

'I'm not secret service, Rogers. I'm a visitor. A photographer.'

He touched his finger to the side of his nose, with that gesture that I always detested. 'I know. I know. Anyway . . .' he paused, '. . . is there something I can do?'

'Yes. I want two seats on any plane tomorrow that's flying to Europe. London. Paris. Anywhere.'

He looked surprised. 'But I thought . . . ah well. I'll see what I can do. Now . . .' he shrugged, '. . . I must get on with the daily grind.'

I closed the door, took Aliki's hand and headed for the street. It had been childish and faintly ridiculous but it had done me a lot of good. As we stepped into the street Aliki laughed softly and said, 'You know you're getting more like a Somali every day.'

'In what way?'

'Suspicious of government employees, unbearably proud and very very touchy.'

'That's me all right.'

There was a note for me back at the hotel. The meeting would be at 7 P.M. and a car would come for us.

The elderly black Lancia called for us at 6.45 and drove us out of town, a few kilometres down the road towards Kismayo. It turned into the gates of a large villa. There was the blue flag of the Somali Republic with its central white star on a flagpole at the gate which was guarded by two soldiers from the Camel Corps. They waved the driver inside and the car parked up at the front of the villa. Shapiro came out smiling and friendly, chatting amiably as he led us into a large room at the back of the villa.

Seated at the magnificent walnut table was Muhammad Siad Barre, Rogers from the consulate, Haji and Issa. We were introduced to the president and then Shapiro waved us to two empty seats before sitting himself. It was Shapiro who opened the meeting. He looked at the president.

'I have told our friend here that London is very grateful for what he has done.'

Haji translated and then the president spoke for several minutes. Haji looked at me.

'The president wishes to add his thanks for what you have done. He is very grateful.'

'What else did he say, Haji?'

Haji looked hesitantly at Shapiro who took the hint and leaned forward towards me, his arms folded. He was trying to look relaxed.

'We've got a problem, Johnny. The president and his ministers have been telling London for several weeks that the *derg* are no longer their own masters and that the Russians are intending to use them as a front for taking over Somalia and then Kenya. London didn't . . . that is, they hoped for some positive indication that would confirm this. The stuff that's coming in through Massawa was almost enough but the Ethiops told our people unofficially that these were intended for use solely against the Eritrean revolutionaries. The kind of material involved was suitable for attacking guerrilla-type ground forces so the *derg* were given the benefit of the doubt. The material you photographed is for a very different ball-game and definitely can't be ignored.'

He looked at me for a response but I said nothing. He looked down at the table, shifting a batch of papers a few inches to one side, then he looked back at me.

'We want to help the Somalis, and to do that we need a bit of help from you. Just a few more days of your time.'

'I'm not interested, Joe. We're going to London the first flight I can get.'

I heard Haji translating for the president and ignored it. It was Rogers who spoke next.

'There would be problems there. She would need an exit visa. They're very difficult to get at the moment.'

'Miss Yassou is a British subject, she doesn't need an exit visa to return to London.'

'I'm afraid she does. She isn't *returning* to London. She's never been to the UK.'

'Who says so?'

144

Rogers half smiled and shrugged. 'The records say so. That means she has to satisfy the Somali government about tax clearances. Security aspects etcetera etcetera.'

'What security aspects?'

He shrugged his shoulders. 'Her contacts in Addis. That sort of thing.'

I looked at Haji and said, 'Is it true what this creep is saying? That unless I cooperate the Somali government will make it difficult for Aliki to leave Somalia?'

Haji sighed. 'I think they're only trying to show how important your cooperation is, Johnny.'

'Like hell they are. They're saying that they'll use illegal pressures on a British national to make me do something I don't intend doing.'

Haji said softly, 'Why not see what it is they want. It's not just us, it's your people too.'

'I'll tell you now, Haji, and you too, Joe, that I wouldn't lift a hand to help you under pressures like this. You can go to hell. And believe me I'll raise real hell when I get back.'

Shapiro held up his hand. 'Hold on, Johnny. Nobody's said these things are going to happen. Rogers here is a diplomat, he's only . . .'

'He's a fucking creep, not a diplomat. He's here to protect British citizens not apply illegal pressures on behalf of a foreign government.'

'OK. Let's just . . .'

'Tell him to leave right now or I'll go back to the hotel and phone the embassy in Nairobi.'

Rogers looked at Shapiro who nodded and waved his hand vaguely in the direction of the door. 'I'll be in touch, Algy.'   .

Rogers was shaking with anger as he stood up and walked to the door, slamming it behind him. Shapiro sighed and looked at Haji.

'You talk to him, Haji. Maybe he'll at least listen to you.'

Haji took a deep breath and then spoke very slowly and

145

very quietly. 'Just ignore Rogers. He's a fool, but he thought he was doing his duty by trying to help the Somali authorities. It was stupid and crude. Nobody had suggested such pressures to him. But he's a bureaucrat and that's the way their minds go if they're third-rate.' He looked at me. 'I'll get him made *persona non grata* if that would mollify you.' He sighed. 'Anyway, back to the real problem. The government here in Mogadishu see their worst fears confirmed. The Ethiopians are going to destroy us. My own men, the guerrillas in the Ogaden will be the excuse. When they have finished with us they will just go straight on south through the Northern Frontier District and down to Nairobi. Then they'll have Mombasa. A real port that can take a Russian fleet that can control the Indian Ocean. The trade of India, Sri Lanka, Japan and Australia will be virtually controlled by Moscow.' Haji spread his hands in resignation. 'Once they move against us with the material in that dump then all we can do is die.' He looked at me. 'Our only hope was that London would believe us and take some action. They didn't believe us but at least Joe Shapiro gave us a chance to change their minds. Your photographs have done that. They believe us now. They are willing to cooperate with us but only unofficially.' He shook his head in doubt. 'And that means you, Johnny. I offered myself but I don't have the knowledge. None of us does. That's all there is to it. We are entirely dependent on you.'

'For what?'

Haji looked at Joe Shapiro who said, 'We would provide the equipment and explosives to blow up the dump or most of it, if you'd go in there again and fix it.'

'You must be out of your mind, Joe. I'm on my way home. The days when I did that sort of thing were over years ago.'

'There isn't anyone else, Johnny.'

'Send someone from SAS or one of the special units, for God's sake.'

'We daren't risk that. That would make it official.'

146

'You mean if they got caught?'

'Yes.'

'But if I get caught you could swear you'd never heard of me and let me rot until they chopped me.'

Haji interrupted. 'We shouldn't see it like that, Johnny. We'd risk as many lives as it took to get you back. I mean that. I swear it, solemnly.'

I shook my head. 'No way, Haji. I'm sorry. I'm not in that business any longer. Haven't been for years.' I turned to Aliki and saw the tears on her cheeks. 'D'you want me to do this, Aliki?' She shook her head and the tears splashed on to the table. I stood up, taking her hand as I looked at Shapiro and Haji. 'Hope you find somebody, Joe.' And I walked us to the door.

The car took us back in silence to the hotel.

We hadn't spoken much, and after we had dinner I walked her down to the jetty and the old lighthouse. It couldn't have been used for at least fifty years but I'd often sat there on the rocks in the old days. As we sat holding hands she said, 'What did Somali Airlines say?'

'There are two seats on a Boeing 707 in four days' time. A direct flight to Rome and a connection to London on Alitalia about three hours later.'

She looked at me, smiling. 'I can't wait to be with you in London.'

'I didn't take the seats. They said they'd hold them until tomorrow midday.'

'Why didn't you take them?'

'Because you cried.'

'Oh Johnny. I was just being stupid. I realized how much it meant to you on one side and them on the other.'

'What does it mean to them?'

'They're Somalis, Johnny. They want to pretend they're part of the modern world. But they're not. Specialists come to teach them how to grow coffee or how to use the rains for growing grass. How to sell more hides. They don't understand any of it. They don't even try to. They

147

don't want to change. They're children who've been children for centuries. They don't want to change or grow up. They dress up in uniforms and call themselves colonels and generals but it's just a game. Most of Haji's men still carry spears, and some have bows and arrows. They can just about cope with those old rifles. The kind you gave them in the war. There's maybe a hundred men who could use a machine gun providing nothing goes wrong. There are a dozen pilots taught by the Russians. They're children, Johnny. Even Haji wouldn't understand how to use explosives. He's a natural leader of tribesmen but for all his Oxford education he never learned about explosives. And the Ethiopians will kill every man, woman and child they can find. And the Russians and the Cubans will help them do it. That's why I cried. For them. And for you.'

The moon was coming up, and the sea was calm and I'd had enough for one day.

'How about we go back to bed?'

'Don't be unhappy, Johnny. I can't bear to see you upset because of me.'

'It's nothing to do with you, honey.'

She smiled. 'It is. If it wasn't for me you would just laugh at them and tell them to go to hell and that would be that.'

I looked at her face in the moonlight. She was as beautiful as when I'd first seen her in Kannassian's bar but her face was thinner, the bones of her cheeks more obvious. Maybe there should be a government health warning about falling for ex-MI6 men who hadn't retired to tending their roses. I had been determined not to give in to their blackmail and I knew I was crazy as I heard myself saying, 'Shall I stay and do it and get it over?'

She shook her head. 'Not for me. Not just because it's my people.'

And for some reason I remembered some phrase in the Bible saying that for the sake of her husband a woman should forsake her family and her people. And as I thought it I knew that it wasn't what I wanted for Aliki. I

148

said quietly, 'I'll contact Shapiro when we get back. A few more days won't matter.'

She nodded. 'There's something I meant to tell you.'

Expecting one more piece of bad news I said, 'And what's that?'

She laughed softly. 'I love you.'

'You cheeky bitch . . . and I love you too. Let's go.'

Aliki went up to our room and I went to reception to use the phone in the kiosk. Shapiro sounded as if I had woken him up.

'Who?' he said.

'How many days will it take, Joe?'

'Jesus, what time is it? . . . four, five days at the most. I've got all the stuff you'll need. There'll be plenty of back-up.'

'I'll call you tomorrow.'

'Thanks. I'm grateful. I really am.'

'You bloody well should be.' He laughed as I hung up.

I looked at my watch. In fact it was only just eleven and as I walked to the main staircase I wondered what Shapiro had in mind and what 'plenty of back-up' would amount to.

As I turned on the first floor for the next flight of stairs somebody whispered, 'Johnny.' I turned and saw a woman. I didn't recognize her at first. It was Sabine Peers, Jonnet's daughter. She was wearing a scarf over her hair and she held the two ends at her chin so that very little of her face was exposed. She hurried towards me and I could see the strain in her eyes as she looked up at my face.

'My father sent me to speak to you. It wasn't possible for him to come himself.'

'What's the trouble?'

'You. He sent me to warn you. He begs you to go back to London. He could arrange flights if they're making problems for you.'

'Warn me about what?'

'He begs you not to become any more involved with Somali affairs. The Russians have twenty thousand Cuban

149

soldiers available and ready. Panov and some others are already in this area. They have Somali friends too. He doesn't want you to get caught up in all this. He wishes that he wasn't involved but it's too late for him to back out now.'

'What makes him think that I'm involved?'

She shrugged. 'You're here. You didn't go back to Addis. You went over the border to Hargeisha. You went to the arms dump. My father knows about that but he hasn't told the Russians about you. They already suspect you, Johnny. And Panov would really like to square his account with you. It wouldn't be just a fist fight.'

'Why should your father be concerned about me?'

'He likes you. He admires you. He's a romantic under all that tough skin. He thinks that you and the girl are a marvellous couple and he doesn't want you to get hurt.'

'Who's going to hurt me?'

'I told you. The Russians. Panov's down here already.'

'Where is he?'

She shrugged. 'I can't say any more. My father just told me to warn you. To beg you not to interfere. That's all I can say.'

'Tell him thank you from me.'

She sighed. 'But you're not going to take his warning?'

'I shall bear it in mind. Thank you for coming to deliver his message. How's Logan?'

'Who?'

'Logan. Your husband.'

'That creep. He's trying to get a flight back to London. Can't wait to get back to his teenage mistress.'

'Tell your father thanks for the warning. See you.'

15

Shapiro, Haji and I drove to the villa on the outskirts of Mogadishu early the next morning. The wide double garage had been piled with equipment. Several hundred pencil fuses and detonators. Miles of connecting wire and dozens of boxes of plastic explosive. I ignored the grenade launchers and the automatic rifles with their boxes of ammunition. They weren't part of my operation.

Somebody had taken my rough layout of the arms dump and laid it carefully over a satellite photograph that gave less detail but clearly showed the whole area and the shape of every individual shed and tent. The inner perimeter wire had been marked in in red ink and the general line of the outer unwired perimeter was shown in green hatching.

We sat at the long trestle table and went over London's list of targets. There were thirty-four and it would take me at least two hours on my own to cover them all. We picked on various targets that were grouped near one another and finally reduced the number of actual target sites to seventeen. It was still too many for the time I would have, but at least it was an indication of priorities. When we had finished I looked across at Joe Shapiro.

'What had you planned for the diversion?'

Shapiro nodded to Haji who took out a crumpled paper, glanced at it and then looked at me.

'I'll take thirty men with me and grenade launchers and automatic rifles. We'll come in from the opposite side in two places.'

'They'd eat you, Haji, they've probably got at least

151

thirty or forty trained soldiers there by now. Cubans. How would you get away?'

Shapiro said, 'We'll supply a helicopter and a pilot. To deliver and to bring back.'

Haji went on. 'If you'll tell them what to do I can give you two intelligent men to help you fix the fuses.'

'Somalis?'

'Yes,' he smiled. 'Or don't you believe Somalis can be intelligent enough to set a simple time-fuse?'

'It's a dangerous game for amateurs, Haji.'

'If you will risk it they will.'

'Have you got anybody in mind?'

'Yes. They speak enough English to do what you tell them.'

'I'll talk to them and see what I think.' I turned to Shapiro. 'When's the chopper available?'

'It's waiting and available now.'

'I'll want two days to go over this carefully with Haji and I'll want to have a few dry runs getting the men on and off the chopper.'

'Just say the word.'

'Has London thought about the consequences of this?'

'Of course. The Russians won't be able to prove who did it. They'll guess that it's London because of the technique, but they won't be able to prove it.' He smiled. 'They'll get the message.'

'And what *is* the message?'

'That we've discovered the arms dump. We know what was in it. We've rumbled what they are up to and we won't have it.'

'They'll know we couldn't have done it without the Somalis cooperating.'

'So what?'

'So they won't bomb London but they can easily bomb Mogadishu, Hargeisha, Berbera, and anywhere else they fancy.'

'We'd have them up in the Security Council in twenty-four hours.'

'For Christ's sake the UN couldn't do a thing. And I doubt if you could even get a resolution condemning them. Nobody'd give a damn. And if you did the Russians would veto it. We'd have hundreds killed and they'd be forgotten in a week.'

Shapiro shrugged. 'President Barre has agreed. He knows what they'll accept. If they did nothing they'd be wiped out anyway when the Russians press the button for an attack in the Ogaden.'

I turned to Haji. 'Does Barre realize what the repercussions could be?'

Haji nodded. 'Yes. He understands.'

'Are you sure?'

Haji hesitated for a moment, then said quietly, 'Yes, I'm sure.'

The rest of that day and the next two days were one long slog. The two Somalis were intelligent, and their English was good enough for what I needed. I went over the old army routines of 'platoon in attack' for Haji who seemed to absorb the basics well enough. I laid down target areas and a field of fire to make sure that they weren't bringing fire down on me and the two Somalis.

I watched Haji and his men clamber into and out of the chopper a dozen times, and it looked just as shambolic the last time as the first time.

Shapiro had got hold of two pairs of walkie-talkies for me. They looked pretty battered but they worked. I picked the best one and gave one to Haji with the others as back-ups, and Haji and I used them a couple of times so that he could handle them easily enough to be able to use them in the dark. They were early models. Just a press-button, a switch for transmit and receive, and a neutral that kept them on permanent receive.

It was almost midnight when Haji drove me back to the hotel and as we sat there for a few moments I was reminded of something.

'Haji. When I asked you if Barre really understood

153

what this operation could lead to you hesitated before you said you were sure that he did. Why did you hesitate?'

Haji sighed. A deep, long sigh. 'London have promised him fighters and missiles, tanks and field guns. And a complete training programme for pilots and gunners. Millions of pounds' worth.'

'He's crazy. When this is over and they've sent their message to Moscow he won't get a damn thing unless he pays for it.'

'There were strong hints that the Americans would be assisting as well.'

'And Barre believes all this?'

'Yes.'

'Do you?'

For a moment he was silent. 'I just don't know, Johnny. I can't really believe it, but I can't believe the British would renege on us after all this and leave us almost defenceless against the Ethiopians and the Russians.'

'My God I hope you're right, Haji. By the way you were right about the two Somalis. They're bright.'

He smiled. 'Good. I'll pick you up at 4.30 A.M. OK?'

'OK.'

There were some very pale Somalis as the chopper lifted off from base. It was a fairly old Aero-Spatiale Super Frelon that had been stripped out to take forty passengers, without seats or toilet. It was camouflaged in tan and green and had no insignia. Its numbers were phoney.

The plane swung in a wide curve out to sea and we clattered our way up the coast past Meregh and Obbia, banking westwards over Ras Hafun, settling slowly to land on the outskirts of Burao. The Ethiopian Air Force regularly carried out surveillance flights that photographed the airstrip at Hargeisha but Burao was too deep behind the frontier to be photographed from across the border.

Haji got his men under cover and then mingled them with a camel caravan. We walked to the local coffee-shop

154

and went over the timing one last time. According to what Shapiro called 'local intelligence sources' it seemed that there was still no real defence force at the dump. Just the security patrol. They were obviously very confident that it wouldn't be attacked by the Somalis. The patrols were more against theft than attack. The Russians and the Cubans were administrators and technical experts, not fighting soldiers.

The helicopter would take us to the far side of the *wadi* and the chopper was to come in again for a quick pick-up three minutes after we sent up the first flare. The two Somalis on my team joined us and I went over my plans again. Shapiro had conjured up four watches and I gave them one for each wrist and we synchronized them as accurately as we could.

Haji and I chatted. He had obviously grown fond of Aliki and he asked if I really was going to marry her.

'Why do you doubt it?'

'I guess for the usual reasons. She's brown and you're white. She's never been anywhere apart from Addis and Mogadishu. Two different cultures and all that stuff.'

'You seem to have survived two different cultures.'

He smiled. 'I haven't really. My father was insistent that I went to England and got a degree. I was the obedient elder son. I wasn't happy in England.'

'Why not?'

'They think *we* are like children, but to me *they* were the children. They want things that they don't need. So many things. The men become slaves just to buy these things and the women are all discontented. Everybody even looks unhappy. Never smiling. Never laughing. They actually pay people to make them laugh. They are not like a tribe. Every man is against all other men. No God, no Muhammad, no believing. Just singing in a church and wearing their best clothes. Children are a nuisance. They pay other people to take care of them and teach them. Old people are a nuisance too. Nobody values their wisdom.

Always people are complaining about their lives but still they are afraid to die.'

I laughed. 'You're making *me* laugh, Haji. It's all pretty true but you've exaggerated.'

'Do you like your culture, your civilization?'

'Some of it. Not all of it. But I don't like everything about Somalis either.'

He smiled. 'Aliki will heal you, my friend.'

I watched the chopper fly off low in the darkness and turned to watch Haji lead off his men. They had already gone, silently into the darkness. They were to have an hour to reach their places and spread out into their groups.

The two Somalis and I walked slowly in the darkness right to the edge of the barbed-wire perimeter about two hundred yards south of where I had gone in before. The night was bitter cold and the canvas packs were heavy and ungainly.

We lay there waiting, my eyes on the luminous hands of my watch. It was already over an hour and I decided to take a risk and cut the wire ready for us to go in. I was barely back with the other two when the red flare went up, hanging in the sky for long moments and then I heard the thud of grenades and we went in through the gap in the wire.

I took each Somali to his target area, prayed that they would remember their instructions and headed off for the crates that were my responsibility. I still had no idea of what was in the crates but apparently London had deciphered the stencilled letters and coded numbers on their sides. There was small-arms and machine-gun fire from the other side of the installation and the satisfactory thud of grenades. I had set all the timers for eighteen minutes and as I finished the last cap I made for my two helpers. It was then I heard the three or four handgun shots quite close. I ran towards our rendezvous point by the howitzers. A white man dressed only in shorts and sandals half turned as I rushed into the tent. He had a Beretta in his hand and one of my Somalis was on the floor. As the man lifted his gun hand I loosed off two rounds at his chest. The slugs stopped him, the force of the second turning his body. The jagged rents in his back where the bullets had exited were enough to know that he was finished. Blood gushed from both wounds as he dropped to his knees and fell forward on to his face.

The Somali had only been hit by one of the man's shots but it had caught him in his neck and he was unconscious, bleeding profusely. The other Somali was kneeling beside him and I pushed him aside as I tore a long strip from the edge of my *shamma*. Padding the cloth I pressed the pad to his wound, tying the strip across his neck in a loop and knotting it under his arm. As I reached down to pick him up I glanced at my watch. It was two minutes to the rendez-vous time and it looked as if I wasn't going to make it. I waved the other Somali to leave me and I could already hear the chopper coming in. The other man shook his head and reached to help me. I brushed his hands away, cursed him and ordered him to leave. He went, resentfully, looking back over his shoulder before he broke into a run. There was still small-arms fire but very desultory and as I straightened up with the wounded Somali over my shoulder I wondered if in fact I might just make the rendezvous before they took off. The pilot had strict orders to leave on time no matter what was happening.

The Somali was lean and hard but surprisingly light and I stumbled out of the tent to where I could see the outline of the chopper in the moonlight. I was about two-thirds of the way there when I felt the blow, as if I had been struck on my leg by a stone. But I'd heard the crack of a rifle and I guessed it was a slug not a stone. But there was no pain yet and I stumbled on through the soft sand.

Ten yards from the plane Haji came flying out with two others and they took the man from my shoulders. The pain was just starting as arms reached down to help me up the metal steps.

The slug had gone deep into the muscle of my thigh and

157

it had obviously nicked an artery. Blood was pulsing out but intermittently and I jammed my thumb deep into my thigh until the bleeding was just seepage. A bullet knocked out a rear observation window as we lifted off and in the general clatter I told Haji how to apply a tourniquet. I hadn't thought of medical supplies and the pain grew almost unbearable as we headed back down the coast. Haji sat alongside me on the metal floor, holding my hand as I tried not to scream.

I was conscious all the while, but even now I can't remember the rest of the journey, the landing, or the trip to the hospital. The first thing I was aware of was nausea from the anaesthetic as I came round. They'd dug out the bullet and cleaned up the wound. The Italian surgeon thought I might have a slight limp but nothing more. The wounded Somali was OK. It was only a flesh wound.

Haji was sitting at the side of the bed, his spaniel eyes on my face.

'I want to thank you, Johnny.'

'Did the dump go up?'

'We could see it from Hargeisha as we flew back. It was an inferno. They could feel the explosions on the ground in Borama. It was a great success.'

'Any casualties with your men?'

'One flesh wound on a man's arm. He's OK. It was almost too easy and one-sided.'

'Good work. Well done.'

Haji smiled. 'Good planning. Good timing. But it wasn't the operation I wanted to thank you for. It was for saving my brother.'

'Your brother?'

He laughed. 'Your two almost intelligent Somalis were my brothers.'

'I gather that it was only superficial.'

'He's alive and he wouldn't be if you'd left him there.'

'Where's Aliki?'

'It's still early morning. I'll go to the hotel and bring her here about ten-thirty or eleven.'

16

The residue of the anaesthetic must have put me to sleep again for when I woke the lights were on and as I looked at my watch it showed 3 A.M. As I turned to take the glass of water on the bedside table I saw a note and leaned over to read it. It was from Haji. He would be back at ten o'clock in the morning.

I slept until the nurse woke me for breakfast. Orange juice and scrambled eggs on toast. It was eight o'clock when the doctor came to check the dressing on my leg. He said it would be possible to walk with a stick in a couple of days provided the antibiotics worked and I kept my weight off the leg.

By ten o'clock Haji had not arrived, neither had Aliki, and it was noon before Haji walked in alone.

'Where's Aliki?'

He was trembling as he stood by the side of the bed looking down at me. His voice was just a whisper.

'She's not there, Johnny. She left the hotel.'

'What's going on?'

'I don't know.'

'Oh, come on. *What's going on?*'

'I went to the hotel yesterday to bring her over to see you. I was there early, about eight. I wanted her to have time to settle down after I'd told her about your leg. She wasn't in the room. Her things were all there. I sat there waiting for over an hour. I went down to the patio but she wasn't there. Then I went back in the foyer and saw the manager. He looked very shifty. I went to reception and asked where she was and the clerk called the manager. He

159

asked me to go to his office. He said she'd left in the middle of the night with two men.' He paused. 'One was a Somali and the other was Panov.'

'How did he know it was Panov?'

'He didn't. But he gave me a good description and it was Panov all right. They took her away in a car.'

'Does Shapiro know this?'

'I don't know.'

'Haven't you asked him what he's doing about it, for Christ's sake?'

There was a long pause, and then Haji said, 'He's left. He's gone back to London.'

'When did he go?'

'Late last night. A plane took him to Nairobi. He was flying to London from there on an East African Airlines scheduled flight.'

'Then he must have known about Aliki before he left.'

'I should think so.'

'Did he know that our raid had been successful?'

'Yes. The president's deputy told him. He said Shapiro seemed very satisfied.'

'And Shapiro didn't raise the subject of Aliki?'

'I was told off the record that it was mentioned to him and he said he already knew.'

'He didn't ask what they were going to do to get her back?'

'I don't think so.'

'The bastard.'

As I swung my legs clumsily out of the bed he said, 'Sit back, Johnny. I've been doing things already.'

'What things?'

'I've seen the president himself. He was very angry. Genuinely angry. There is nothing official or diplomatic he can do. If he raises an official complaint with the Russian Embassy in Addis or even direct to Moscow they will either deny it or ignore it. He's disgusted with Shapiro and he believes now that London have just used him, and you as well, and that they don't intend keeping their

160

promises about arms and training. He is ready to see you any time you want and he has told me that I can have up to fifty trained Camel Corps soldiers and any weapons we've got, to get her back.'

'D'you think they could have got her out of the country by now?'

'The president ordered a watch to be kept at the airfield and ports but you know what it's like, we don't have recognizable frontiers. It would be easy to get her out.'

'Is Jonnet still at the hotel?'

'He wasn't staying there. He's got a house just outside the town. That's where he usually stays. D'you think he's in this?'

I shrugged. 'He sent me the warning. I thought it was just a threat against me. It never entered my mind that they'd involve Aliki. Do you know Jonnet's place?'

'Yes. I can take you there.'

'Let me get dressed. Can you get me a gun? Two guns. A machine rifle. Say a Kalashnikov or an AKM, and a handgun. I'll wait for you here. OK?'

Haji nodded and left, obviously reluctantly.

Despite all that training and experience those years ago I was on the edge of panic. If it had not been Aliki I'm sure that I would have known right away what to do. But it *was* Aliki and my thinking was hopelessly confused. What did they hope to gain? Kidnapping her could only affect me, and hurting me could hardly be worth openly offending the Somali government. But their motive was less important than finding where she was.

They could have taken her over the border into the Ogaden by hundreds of unmarked, unguarded desert tracks, they could have taken her south to the Northern Frontier District. She could be across the Red Sea by now in Marxist Yemen. There were scores of Somali dhow captains who were used to running arms and contraband to the Yemeni coast. They could have used a light plane to take her to Addis, or she could still be in or near Mogadishu. Maybe working out their motivation would give a clue to where they were holding her.

I needed somewhere I could think. I needed someone who could help me think. And I thought of Shapiro. Why had he left knowing that they'd taken Aliki? And why no message for me about the operation on the arms dump?

Then Haji came back. He'd got a newish Thompson and a PO8 Luger wrapped up in a monkeyskin.

'Haji, I want a house, or some place where I can work things out. How do we find one? And I need a phone.'

'In town it's not possible but out on the fringes . . .' he held up his hand. '. . . No. There is a place. Near the barracks and it's got a phone. I'll take you there and we can pick up your kit from the hotel on the way there.'

I went into the hotel with him. The bill had been paid but the police had made them leave the room locked. I paid to keep the room for another month in case Aliki came back. As I scribbled a note for her I turned to Haji.

'What's the name of the villa?'

'Villa dei Fiori. Any taxi driver will know where it is.'

I gave the note to the manager to give to her if she came.

The villa looked peaceful and friendly in the late afternoon sun. All the usual bougainvillaea, mimosa and hibiscus around the front patio, and inside it was surprisingly cool. The furnishings were high-grade Italian colonial and there was a high-walled garden at the rear. The villas each side were both too far away to overlook us.

The first thing I did was look for the phone and check that it was working. It was.

It took me an hour to get through to London. Joe Shapiro wasn't in his office and they didn't know where he could be contacted. It was one of those firm, decisive twin-set and pearls voices. She had recognized my name straight away and she'd obviously been briefed not to put me through and to give nothing away. She didn't know when he would be available. I was getting the brush-off Mark II. With Mark I the guy actually spoke to you and politely and diplomatically made clear that whatever you wanted wasn't on. They were polite and diplomatic because they had worked out that you were worth the time and trouble and they might need you some time in the future. You got Mark II when they'd washed their hands of you. If you had ever been part of the setup you got the message. Your arse was out in the snow. There was going to be no help from London.

I asked Haji to try and get through to Barre and get him to try and contact Shapiro and put top-level pressure on in London. He came back twenty minutes later. Barre had phoned London and asked for the Foreign Minister and had ended up with a glorified clerk. When he had raised hell and demanded to speak to Shapiro he had been put through to him. When Barre had said his piece about me and Aliki, Shapiro had said that he'd never heard of me. If a John Grant was in trouble and was a British national he suggested that he should seek help in the normal way through HM Consul in Mogadishu. The message from London couldn't be clearer.

What foxed me was that when London threw you to the wolves you generally knew why or could guess why. And for the life of me I couldn't guess why they were cutting me out. Usually it was because you'd broken one of the rules, written or unwritten, or gone too far, or just made a cockup that left pieces lying around. But none of that applied in this case. I'd done everything they'd asked and I wasn't one of their stooges for Christ's sake.

When Haji came back I asked him about the car. 'Did anyone take the number of the car or give a description of it?'

'No. People don't think that way here. It was black but practically every car in Mogadishu's black.'

'What about the Somali? Did anybody recognize him?'

'No. They said he was young and looked like a Turkana from the border but they could be wrong. They weren't suspicious. It all looked normal to them until she didn't come back.'

163

'Will the police be any use?'

Haji shrugged. 'I don't think so. They're not used to European crime. They catch thieves and camel-rustlers. A few Somali murderers, but they're not trained for sophisticated crime.'

'Do they have informers?'

'Yes, hundreds.'

'Can we use them?'

'Yes. I'll get the president's secretary to phone the Chief of Police.'

Haji talked for a long time on the phone and when he hung up he looked disturbed.

'Won't they cooperate, Haji?'

'Yes they'll cooperate OK. He's phoning them now.'

'Why so gloomy?'

He sat down in one of the leather armchairs, taking a deep breath before he turned to look at me.

'The Ethiopians have started the war. The fighting started just outside Jigjiga. The first reports say there are at least two thousand Cuban troops with the Ethiopians. There are hundreds of my men dead already. They're using light tanks, flame throwers, howitzers and they've got complete control of the air. The president's in a meeting now to decide whether he should order the Somali army into the fight to save my people.'

'Do you want to go up to them?'

'It's too late, Johnny. It's not a war. It's genocide. I've asked the president to tell my men to stop fighting and get back inside our borders. I couldn't have made any difference if I had been there. We're a guerrilla force not an army. What can rifles and a few machine guns do against artillery and modern fighter-bombers? There are other leaders with them who can take charge. I'm a politician not a soldier. Better leave it to the warriors.'

'I'm sorry, Haji. Are you sure you want to spend your valuable time with me?'

'I'll stay until we've got Aliki back, Johnny, don't worry

about anything else. What do you want with the police informers?'

'Ask them about any gossip concerning the Russian mission. A new face. Anything strange that's been happening in the last few days. People going off in cars in unusual directions. Men buying food and stores. Anything. Give them the description of the Somali and Panov.'

He was on the telephone for half an hour. Sometimes calm, sometimes angry, and frequently mentioning the president's name.

It was past midnight when I had the first useful thought. Jonnet had sent his daughter to warn me or threaten me. Saying that they'd want to level the score. I'd assumed that he meant that they would try to kill me. And I'd assumed wrong. Taking Aliki was a shrewd, ruthless blow and I ought to have thought of it and given her protection. But if Jonnet knew enough to warn me then it was possible that he not only knew what they were intending to do but where they had taken her.

I tried it out on Haji and he agreed, but he seemed preoccupied and I assumed his mind was with his men.

Then he said quietly, 'You have thought of the worst possibility?'

'What's that?'

He sighed. 'That they kill her.'

'They could have killed her at the hotel.'

'Yes, of course. But this way they turn the knife in you as well. They leave you so that you never know. Get rid of her body and leave you to sweat it out for days, months or years according to your feelings for her.'

It had already all gone through my mind but I'd not let it work into my thinking. 'How about we go and visit Jonnet?'

'Now? It's nearly one o'clock.'

'Just the time to pressure him.'

'OK. If you want the gun and ammunition they're in the boot of the car.'

'The Luger will be enough.'

165

Jonnet's place was on the other side of town and I got Haji to drive past a couple of times so that I could look it over. It looked as if our visit wasn't going to be a surprise. There were lights on all over the house, and the entrance and the front of the house were floodlit. And a man with a rifle stood, smoking a cigarette, in the shadow of the big wrought-iron gates. He wasn't a Somali. He was a white man, but a very dark white man and I guessed he was a Cuban. We parked the car a hundred yards away and I sat there working it out.

'Would a man like Jonnet normally have a guard on his house?'

'Not a real guard, and certainly not armed. He'd have a night-watchman, probably the garden-boy, and he'd be asleep most of the time. Local thieves would leave Jonnet alone because they'd know that the police wouldn't rest until they were caught.'

'OK. You stay here Haji and I'll do a recce round the house and come back. Say half an hour.'

I checked the spring and the bullets in the Luger's chamber and then pushed it back into place until it clicked home. It was an awkward weapon for a pocket with its extra long barrel but I didn't expect to have to use it.

I went in over the ornate railings at the side of the house and stood under a palm to look at the villa. There were lights in all the downstairs rooms at the back but only one of the upper rooms was lit. A faint glow that was probably a bedside lamp.

It looked as if the man at the front was the only guard and I made my way slowly along the side of the villa. He was lighting a cigarette and the rifle was leaning propped against a stone urn holding trailing geraniums. He looked casually towards the house and then back to the street.

I turned back. It would be easier to approach him from the far side where the trees would give me cover. But I needed to see what was going on inside the villa before I made a move.

The first room was a well laid out kitchen with modern

appliances, the second was a dining-room with a table that would take twelve or fourteen people and the last room was obviously the living-room, expensively and elegantly furnished but obviously lived in. All the rooms were empty. The lights were obviously only for security.

I went back for Haji and gave him the Luger, posting him near the front door of the house to cover me on my way up to the guard.

When I was within five feet of him I could hear him singing softly to himself. I didn't recognize the tune but the words were enough – *amigas, palomas, noches* and *quieros* were much featured. He didn't move until I was right behind him, and he was far too slow. I clamped one hand over his mouth and pressed the nerve centre under his ear with my other thumb. He sagged so easily and quickly that I thought for a moment he was faking, but he wasn't. He was out, and he wouldn't be a problem for at least an hour or so. Haji helped me to drag him into the bushes and I took the bolt from his rifle and slung it into the darkness of the garden.

The big carved front door wasn't locked and we went quickly into the tiled hall and up the stairs. Jonnet was in the first bedroom I tried. The one with the dim light. He was asleep, one hand outside the single sheet, still resting on an open paperback. It was the French version of *The Spy Who Came in from the Cold*. He was breathing stertorously, his mouth wide open, his pale face showing a network of veins around his nose and mouth. He stirred only slowly as I shook his shoulder and I glanced at the bedside table and saw the bottle of Valium capsules.

It took several minutes to wake him but once his eyes opened I pulled him up by his pyjama jacket and, mouth still gaping, he tried to take in what was happening. Jonnet wasn't used to being on the receiving end of trouble. He wasn't expecting me because he peered at my face as he said, 'Who are you? What do you want?'

'It's Grant, Jonnet. I want Aliki. Where is she?'

His chest was heaving as he looked up at me and he was

167

very scared. There were bubbles of saliva on his flabby lips as he spoke. 'I can't help you.' He shook his head slowly in confirmation and then he cried out as I tore off the sheet and swung his legs to the floor.

'Stand up, Jonnet.'

He stood up slowly, his legs trembling, and then he saw Haji and the Luger and he collapsed back on to the bed. I pulled him back to a sitting position and bent down with my face near his.

'Tell me what you know, Jonnet, or you're going to get hurt.'

'I can't help you,' he whispered. 'Nothing to say.'

I reached out for the Luger and took it from Haji without looking away from Jonnet's face, and he moaned as I rammed it against his cheekbone. 'Where is she, Jonnet?'

He groaned as tears filled his eyes. 'I don't know. I swear I don't know.'

'You sent me a warning, you must have known what they were planning.'

'I knew they would take her. I warned you, Grant. I didn't want it to happen. You took no notice. You left her unprotected.'

'So where is she?'

'In God's name I don't know.'

'What do they intend doing with her?'

His chest was heaving as he fought for breath. 'They . . . want . . . you. They'll exchange her for you.'

'Is that what they told you?'

'Yes . . . some water . . . please.'

'When you've told me more.'

'There's nothing more to tell.'

'If they wanted me why didn't they wait for me?'

He shrugged. 'They expect you to resist and maybe you are killed.'

'Why should they worry about me being killed?'

The pale washed-out blue eyes in the flabby face looked at me. 'They said they want you for diplomatic reasons.'

'What diplomatic reasons?'

'I don't know. I don't know how their minds work. Panov was scared and angry. He was in trouble from Moscow about what you did at the arms dump. He flew straight down here. I was already here on business. He was in a hurry to square things with Moscow.'

'You mean Moscow authorized the kidnapping of Aliki?'

'I don't know, Grant. I swear I don't know. I was no longer in favour. No longer in the confidence of Panov.'

'And when they said they wanted me for diplomatic reasons didn't you ask what they meant?'

'Yes, of course. Panov just shrugged and smiled.'

'Why didn't they leave a note for me saying they would exchange her for me?'

'There are other ways to contact you.'

'They don't know where I am.'

'They can find out. They have informers here. They can leave a message for you at the hotel.'

We trussed him up with the bedsheets and talked on the landing outside his bedroom. We both thought he was telling the truth but neither of us was absolutely sure. We decided to take Jonnet with us. I had no idea what we could do with him but it seemed like squaring things up. Haji watched him dress and I brought down the car to the gates. We were back at the Villa dei Fiori fifteen minutes later.

The words 'diplomatic reasons' kept going through my mind. I had no idea what they could mean. Maybe they were under the impression that if they got me they could trade me for something they wanted from London. But if they had checked with their people in London they would know that there was no chance of a deal. Shapiro would have laughed in their faces if they propositioned him about exchanging me for some KGB man in the Scrubs, no matter how lowly he was. There was no other diplomacy that sprang to mind.

I slept until eight o'clock and Haji had got hold of a

Camel Corps *syce* as a cook and I had scrambled eggs and coffee to keep the machinery working. Haji had been up and around for hours and joined me at the table for a coffee. As he sipped it he said, 'Jonnet doesn't know any more than he's told us, Johnny. I'm sure of that now.'

'Why now? What's changed?'

He smiled. 'I gave him a little Somali persuasion. We might as well send him back to his place. He's a sick man. He needs a doctor.'

I went upstairs to have a look at Jonnet. He was lying naked on the bed, his arms tied behind his back. His face was bruised and there was dried blood round his mouth and on his chest. And his swollen scrotum was as big as a coconut. His pale blue eyes were bloodshot and he gave soft animal cries of fear as I leaned over to release his arms. Jonnet wasn't the stuff that heroes are made of and Haji was right. After that treatment he would have talked if he had anything more to say. And I wasn't the stuff that heroes are made of either or I wouldn't have had that twinge of regret as I looked at the man who had given Aliki that little gold cross. It was a bribe of sorts but it had been sentimentally chosen.

I went back downstairs and Haji drove Jonnet back to his villa. There was no sign of the guard, but there were two Somali servants there who took charge of him.

The phone rang a few minutes after Haji's return. It was the police and he talked for a long time, asking questions and listening carefully as I waited impatiently for him to translate for me. When he hung up he said, 'Nothing solid but a fair ragbag of odd pieces.'

'Tell me.'

He sat down. 'The car they used was an old Lancia owned by one of the Russians at their mission. But he left for Moscow two months ago. Two white men, in a car, strangers, bought fruit and bread at a stall on the outskirts of town on the road to Bulo Burti. No description of men or car. The police have heard that Jonnet's place had been broken into last night. None of the more piratical dhows

170

has been hired and to confuse things no car has gone through the check at Bulo Burti township where the metalled road gives way to the desert tracks to the Ogaden.

'According to the police chief himself there are thousands of refugees heading for Mogadishu and the Camel Corps are being used to mark out camps and erect tents for hospitals. And units of the Somali army have been seen heading in convoys towards the Ogaden border.' Haji sighed. 'Sending in the army will give my men a chance to retreat and the women and children to escape, but it won't hold the Ethiopians and Cubans back for long. It was a gesture that will keep Barre in power . . . but it will sink him internationally. It's a real disaster.'

'Do you think blowing up the dump made them start?'

He shrugged. 'I don't think so. It was there to be used. It may have given them an excuse but that's all. But it could limit how far they'll go.'

Then the phone rang again. I answered it but nobody spoke. It was the Mogadishu version of the heavy breather.

Half an hour later a car stopped outside. A man got out, came through the gate and walked up the path.

The last person I'd expected to see was Logan Peers. He was wearing a bush jacket and shorts, and his knees were strangely white. He walked in, sat himself down without being invited and said, 'I've been asked to deliver a message to you.'

I didn't reply and he went on. 'I must say that I'm deeply shocked and disgusted at what your people have done to poor old Jonnet. I've already lodged an official complaint with the president himself. He's going to get the police to take appropriate action against the lot of you. However that isn't the purpose of this visit.' He paused to glare at me. 'You can't have expected that they wouldn't retaliate, so you won't be surprised at what's happened. Anyway, the long and short of it is that they'll trade your girlfriend for you. I recommend that you agree right

171

away.' He paused for significance. 'She's a very attractive girl and the Cubans can have nasty ways with pretty prisoners.'

'Has anyone ever told you that you're a shit, Peers?'

'Not that I recall. Abuse won't help you of course.'

'What do they want with me?'

He grinned. 'Your guess is as good as mine. Passport photographs maybe.'

'Are you still with SIS?'

'Kind of. On the fringes let's say.'

'Where do they want to do the exchange?'

'At their place. I'll inform you where it is. You just go there and they'll release the girl.'

'Like fuck they will.'

'Has anyone ever told you that you're a vulgar man, Grant? A ruffian masquerading as a knight in armour. You never understood what makes things tick, did you? Not even when you were SIS playing Robin Hood in Addis. The sea-green incorruptible strutting to the gallery, admired by one and all, friends and enemies alike. You're a phoney, Johnny Grant. And very naïve if you didn't think they'd pick up the girl and hold her hostage. Maybe you've had enough of her by now.'

I looked across at him, and it was several minutes before I could speak, as he looked back defiantly.

'How can I contact them?'

'Jonnet's phone number's 57. Just ask for me when you're ready to go.'

'I'll do that.'

He stood up and walked to the door, closing it quietly behind him, satisfied that he'd put me down.

The sound of Peers's departing car had barely died away when one of Haji's brothers walked in from the garden at the back. He was smiling, and said something in Somali to Haji who looked pleased.

'They've traced her, Johnny. They know where she is. They've actually seen her. My other brother is still there keeping watch on the place.'

'How did they find her?'

'Barre told the Russians at their mission that they have to leave by today. There's only seven of them but apparently Moscow aren't at all pleased, they've tried desperately to keep a door open with us despite supporting the Ethiopians. Barre told them about Panov and his extracurricular activities down here. He's got no authority to be here. No visa. Nothing. When they radioed Moscow why they were being thrown out, it seems Moscow ordered them to contact Panov. Abdi was watching the mission and when a car headed out in a hurry he followed it, and stopped short when he saw it heading for this remote villa.'

'Where is it?'

'It's down south at Merca, not far from the sea. It's isolated. Nothing near it for miles.'

'How many were there?'

Haji spoke to his brother and then translated for me.

'Panov is there. Three Cubans and two Somalis. There may be more but that's all they've seen.'

'Tell him how grateful I am, Haji.'

He laughed. 'Tell him yourself, he speaks English.'

And I said my thanks to his brother, conscious of having made one more European gaffe of condescension. I knew his other brother spoke some English but had assumed that this one didn't.

Haji's brother drew out a rough map of the route to Merca and then the location of the villa.

The house was long and narrow. Six rooms plus a bathroom and a kitchen with a leg on one end that had previously been the servants' quarters. That's where Aliki was held. His brother had seen her face several times at the window. There was no cover in any direction on the approaches to the house, and there was no garden. Just an L-shaped building set in acres of sand. Electricity from a petrol generator, and water supplied by tanker to underground cisterns. The building had originally been built to house a small detachment of Italian troops.

173

I turned to Haji. 'What help can we get? Men and weapons?'

'I think Barre will say you can have whatever you need. Tell me what you want and I'll phone his secretary.'

I reckoned that we should need twenty men as an assault group and at least half of them should be trained soldiers or at least Camel Corps regulars. Two heavy machine guns, automatic rifles and a couple of grenade launchers. Haji phoned through my shopping list and despite their desperate situation he was told that I was to have whatever I needed. No helicopters were available, the dozen they had were all in the fighting zone bringing out refugees but there was a private chopper owned by a Swedish pilot and that was available for hire.

We traced the Swede who had the chopper and he was willing to pilot for me provided I paid the going rate plus war zone insurance. I fixed to see him early the next morning and then I turned in. I was exhausted, and the pain in my leg had been almost unbearable. I took half a dozen painkillers and a swig of brandy and lay back on the bed trying not to think of Aliki.

17

I picked out four grenade launchers and checked the fuses in the grenades. Some were covered with rust but still usable, a few were in too dangerous a state to use. But there were enough for my operation.

There was no winch on the chopper so I would have to use a knotted rope. I got a camouflage uniform and a pair of rubber-soled shoes and we made one practice run with the chopper. He was a good pilot and he landed me softly but the pain in my leg was bad. Haji got me a real pain-killing shot from the hospital that would keep the pain at bay for three hours. I'd have to take it before we took off.

Haji had 'borrowed' six NCOs from the Camel Corps who had had good training in using the grenade launchers and I showed them on the roughly drawn plan the sites for the launchers and the targets.

If it wasn't Aliki the bastards were holding I'd have made Haji's men practise for at least a week until every move was timed and coordinated and every target vectored and ranged. But it *was* Aliki, and I couldn't bear to think of what they'd do to her. Haji didn't know much about that old relationship and somehow I couldn't bring myself to tell him.

I was beginning to feel weaker as we went over the routines of synchronizing watches. Torch signals and call signs on the radios. I needed a second-in-command who could do all that for me. Haji could give me a thoughtful comparison of the advantages of Keynesian finance versus *laissez-faire* but he didn't know one end of a grenade from the other, or how to organize the preliminaries of even a small raiding party. It wasn't that my mind was becoming more confused, it was that it was getting clearer every minute as my physical strength seemed to be ebbing away. And what my mind made so clear I didn't like.

I had no cards in my hand. They must have known that I might trace them and could half expect me to be coming in, so there was no element of complete surprise. They had Aliki so we couldn't just blow the place to pieces. As the sun went down it looked as if the good Lord was on my side. The sky was clear and the moon was full.

Haji went off with his men and the equipment in the big Cape trucks left over from World War II. I gave them two hours and then we took off. No navigation lights and no lights inside the cabin apart from the shaded lights on the instrument panel. We were over the area ten minutes later. A mile from the house we came down low and I saw the brief flash from Haji's torch. They were already in place. Waiting for me, and my signal light.

Panov and his people would be able to hear the chopper but they wouldn't be able to see even its silhouette until it passed between them and the moon. By then it would be at about seven hundred feet if my calculations were correct. They would hear that it hadn't landed, and if luck was on my side they'd take it for no more than a routine reconnaissance of the coast because of the Ethiopians. That was what I hoped.

The night air was bitterly cold as I slid back the door, gripping the rope with one hand as I sat down. As the chopper banked I gripped the rope with both hands and found a knot for my feet.

As the rope swung free from the fuselage I lowered myself knot by knot. Counting as I went. At number twenty I stopped and looked down into the cloud of sand from the chopper's blades. Then I let go. I dropped less than four feet and the rope snaked along the ground for a moment then disappeared.

I lay on the ground and waited for the sand to settle. Five minutes later I could make out the lights from the house and I looked through the night-glasses. There were lights on in all the windows except one and an outside light on the narrow patio at the side of the front door.

There seemed to be no guard outside the house, which fitted in with the information we had from Haji's men. But there was probably a lookout in the room without a light. I looked at my watch. There was just over ten minutes before Haji could expect me to fire the first flare. It was time to get on my way.

I crawled to about twenty metres from the villa. The side of the extension where they were holding Aliki was half in shadow and there was the faint sound of music from the front of the villa. A Latin-American samba. I stood up and moved slowly towards the shadow, crouching as I went forward. The only window to the extension was at the rear. It was barred and fly-meshed but all I needed to do was attract Aliki's attention so that she could take cover on the floor when the grenades came roaring in on the far side of the villa to open up an entrance for Haji's men.

I looked at my watch. There were three minutes to go before I fired the Very pistol that would get Haji started, and I moved towards the rear corner of the house. As I peered cautiously round the corner I could see the back of the villa bright from the light of the moon. I heard the swish of whatever it was that hit me and the grunt of the man as he rolled on to me from the low flat roof of the extension. The club or whatever it was had missed my skull and smashed across my neck. It didn't stun me but I stood for a moment paralysed and the man's arms went round me pinioning my arms to my sides. As I struggled instinctively I realized that I couldn't move my right arm at all because the blow had made it useless. A rough voice said softly, '*Se tranquilo amico*,' and I felt the nose of the handgun against my spine as he pushed me forward.

Panov was standing at the open door, smiling, a pistol in his hand, and he moved aside as I was shoved into the kitchen, through a narrow corridor into a large bedroom. The Cuban dumped my small canvas holdall on a small table and Panov waved me towards a wooden chair. There were slow spasms of pain from my neck to my fingers as if there was too much blood trying to pump through my veins. But I could hear and see.

Panov sat on the bed facing me, his sallow face thinner than I remembered, his eyes watching me as the Cuban roped my arms and ankles to the chair.

'I sure you come, comrade Grant,' he grinned. 'I tell her every day. He come for you today or tomorrow. Very soon he come.' He leaned forward. 'We do a deal, yes? You sign document and we let her go.'

'What do you want me to sign?' And my voice seemed to be coming from the ceiling, echoing and reverberating in my head.

'Just very simple paper. You sign that you are spy for British gov'ment. They instruct you to blow up Ethiopian arms store with help of Somali gov'ment and their armed forces.'

And then I realized what 'diplomatic reasons' meant. If I signed such a document they could offer it to the world's press and the United Nations as proof that their attack on the Somalis was only a legitimate reaction to an act of war by the Somalis, encouraged and assisted by the British.

No wonder Shapiro had sloped off so quickly and denied all knowledge of me, even to President Barre. He had guessed why Panov had kidnapped Aliki. It seemed obvious now even to me.

I wondered how long it would be before Haji realized that something had gone wrong and came in without my signal. It was already several minutes overdue and Panov didn't seem to be aware that it wasn't just me. I shook my head as I looked back at him.

'Forget it, Panov. The deal you asked for was to have me, and you'd let the girl go free. That's the message I got from Logan Peers.'

He shrugged, smiling, his arms outstretched. 'Of

course. Of course. But you not say yes. You not come here to give yourself up for the girl. You come here to rescue her, yes? Typical British bad faith, yes?'

'Let her go, Panov, and I'll stay.'

'And you sign statement?'

'No.'

He grinned. 'But it is true statement, no? You blow up arms stores for British with Somali help. True or false?'

'Forget it, Panov. It's just me for the girl.'

'Nothing would change your mind?'

'Nothing.'

He grinned. 'You quite sure?'

I didn't answer and he spoke in Spanish to the Cuban who looked at me for a moment and then left the room. Panov sat looking at me, smiling, only turning his head as the door opened.

Two different Cubans came in and two Somalis. Then Aliki followed by the first Cuban. Aliki was naked, her eyes closed as they pushed her on to the bed.

Panov grinned. 'They like having her, comrade. Maybe she like it too.' He turned to watch as the two Cubans took off their trousers and climbed on the bed alongside her. Panov turned back to look at me. 'You tell me when you think she had enough and you change your mind. After the Cubans there's the two Somalis.'

I closed my eyes and tried not to listen. The chair went over with me as I struggled to get free and Panov was standing over me, grinning down at me as I lay helpless on my back. His heavy boot was over my face when the first grenade hit the house. Then another, and another and then Haji's men came pouring in, screaming, firing hosepipe in all directions, and it was a miracle that anybody in that room survived. When Haji cut me free the Cubans and the two Somalis were all dead. I saw one of Haji's brothers take off his *shamma* and hand it to Aliki. Panov by some miracle was still alive.

Haji said softly, 'They'll look after Aliki, she wasn't hit.

179

She'll be OK.' I wondered if he knew what they had done to her. He stood there, his soft brown eyes looking at my face, and I knew then that he did know.

I reached out my hand for the knife he was holding in his left hand and as I took it he turned away, closing the door behind him as he left me alone with Panov.

He was leaning forward, arms outstretched, his legs bent in a wrestler's crouch, sweat pouring down his face. The knife caught his wrist as I slashed the first time and he put one hand up to protect his face as I moved nearer. He sprang at me, his hand trying to grab mine, his knee jabbing again and again at my groin, and then he sighed as the knife went into his chest, and his body hung on me like a dead-weight, sliding down to his knees, one arm and his head resting on the mattress of the bed as if he was just sleeping. I ripped open his khaki green shirt. There was blood pumping from the left side of his brown hairy chest. He opened his eyes slowly as I pulled off his shirt, his lips set in a rictus of pain, and I looked at his face as I slid the knife into him between his ribs. The complex of muscles spasmed as I used both hands to drag the knife down his belly until it jarred against his pelvic bone. And I watched his face as the blood drained from his belly until the stench of his guts was too much.

I stood up, trembling, my hand clutching the table for support, my head hanging down and I was still there when Haji found me. As I straightened up I saw him glance briefly at Panov's body lying in a pool of blood and then he looked back at my face.

'I've sent her off to the hospital, Johnny. She needs a sedative . . . she'll be all right.' He took my arm. 'I've got one of the trucks outside. I'll take you back.'

'Who's with Aliki?'

'Both my brothers. They'll see she's properly treated at the hospital.'

'Take me to see her.'

'You need a rest, Johnny. You need to wind down. Then you can see her.'

I shook my head and it felt as heavy as lead. 'I want to be with her. Take me now.'

Even in the fresh dawn air I could smell the reek of cordite. The mortars had taken out the whole of the end wall of the villa. I should have thought of the flat roof over the extension. In the old days it would have been so obvious.

18

By the end of a week the bruises on Aliki's face and body had faded but the bruised mind was going to take much longer. After two weeks in the sun, swimming slowly in the pool and just lounging around she was beginning to relax. She could mouth words even though no sounds came out. She wanted to speak and that cheered me up a lot.

When you have a problem like this there's a tendency to contrive situations that make the mute person speak. Situations of surprise or pleasure or even excitement. And a tendency to attach too much importance to the first words spoken. In fact the first word Aliki uttered was 'no' when a new houseboy went to pour cream in her coffee. And when she realized she had spoken she looked at me, smiling, and tried to speak again but it wouldn't come out. It was another week before the dam broke. She could speak again. Quite fluently. But she had difficulty with words beginning with S and T. It was an impediment but it no longer stopped us from talking. I found it painful to watch her struggling to get out some word, longing to say it for her, but knowing that that would make it worse.

I had kept in touch with the studio every three or four days and Hugo seemed to be coping well enough. Some clients had gone elsewhere when they found I wasn't available but there was more than enough to keep them busy.

At the end of the month I booked us flights to Nairobi and from there to London. It was time to be getting back to real life again.

Until we were walking across the tarmac at the airfield I hadn't realized how much I was going to miss Haji and the rest of them. There were twenty or so walking with us, all regulations abandoned, and as we stood at the top of the aircraft steps to wave to them I felt a strange twinge of sadness. They were like children, happy that we were happy. White teeth, broad smiles, constant wavings of their brown arms and all the restless body movements that you see in any upper-class London disco. Eventually the stewardess asked us to go to our seats. And after one last wave the aircraft door was closed.

On our seats were two small packages, one marked for Aliki and one for me. After the plane was airborne Aliki opened hers. It was a beautifully made wooden box and inside was a honeycomb. She turned to me, smiling. 'It's what a father in my father's people gives his favourite daughter on her marriage day. What's your present?' I opened my package. Wrapped carefully in a piece of pale blue silk were two leather rings about three inches diameter, hair on the outside. Aliki looked pleased. 'Do you know what they are?'

'No.'

'They're a pair of goatskin anklets that they give to a warrior in a *moran* that has fought particularly well to defend the tribe. They're very special.'

19

We had a two-hour stopover in Rome and I bought Aliki a caseful of clothes and bits and pieces. We had to buy an extra case to hold them.

It was grey and raining when we landed at Heathrow and Aliki thought it was wonderful to have rain in the middle of 'the dry season'. She always called summer 'the dry season'.

I ought to have expected it but I hadn't. The hassle started at Immigration. We both went to the queue for British passport-holders. I went through first and stood waiting for them to check Aliki's passport. I realized that something was wrong when he reached for the checklist. His finger went down the list of names and then stopped. He reached for the phone, turning away as he spoke so that I couldn't hear what he said. When he hung up he turned to Aliki.

'Would you just stand aside, miss.' He pointed back to the white-painted queue line. 'Somebody's coming over to see you.'

'What's wrong, officer?'

He looked at me. 'You've been cleared, Mr Grant.'

'Why hasn't Miss Yassou been cleared?'

'Is she related to you?'

'She's my fiancée.'

'Somebody's coming over to interview her.'

'Why. What's the problem?

'I can't discuss it with you.'

'Why not?'

'If you're not her next of kin you've no standing in the matter.'

He turned as a man walked up to his desk. Brown suit, brown shoes and sparse red hair. He reached for Aliki's passport and went through it slowly, page by page including the blank ones. He closed it and waved it towards Aliki, signalling her to go past the desk. As she came through I took her hand and brown suit raised his eyebrows. He turned to Aliki.

'We've got to ask you a few questions, Miss Yassou, let's go to my office.' He turned to me. 'Perhaps you'd care to get a cup of coffee while we talk to Miss Yassou.'

'I'll be with her in your office.'

'I'm afraid that isn't possible.'

'Don't be afraid because she doesn't move from here unless I go with her.'

'You're Mr Grant?'

'That's right.'

'You should know better than make threats, Mr Grant.'

'I'm not making threats. Are you detaining Miss Yassou?'

'I don't know. We'll have to see. I must say your attitude is not helping her.'

'Do you want me to call my lawyer?'

He smiled. 'It's Saturday, Mr Grant.'

'He's got a home and he doesn't play golf. He can be here in half an hour.'

He nodded knowingly. 'You're a bit of a troublemaker from what I hear, Mr Grant. I'd advise you to calm down.'

'What's your name?'

'Ogden, Mr Grant. Victor Ogden.'

'Well, Mr Ogden. Either I go with Miss Yassou or I call my solicitor. You choose.'

For a few moments he tried staring me out. The 'I know your guilty secrets' ploy. Then he sighed. 'It won't be any use, Mr Grant, but by all means come with her.'

Two hours later we were collecting our stuff from the pile by the carousel. When he started on Aliki's passport I

185

was scared that the bastards at the embassy in Addis had made it temporary or conditional or had deliberately made it invalid some way. But it was valid all right. He went through every entry, querying the spelling of her name, her date of birth, why she was visiting the UK. The lot. Her stutter got worse and worse and I was sweating with anger. It was just harassment and it had been laid on specially for me. An official welcome home that said if I talked about what I'd been doing, to the press or anyone else, there would be more to come. I'd seen it all before but there was at least the excuse of being at war in those days. And it hadn't been me.

I took a taxi to Ebury Street and the flat looked as if I'd never left it, apart from a pile of mail. Mrs Marsden had obviously done her stuff while I was away.

Aliki put on one of her new dresses and we drove to the Hilton. A lot of eyes lingered on her as we ate.

We had been in London for two months and I found it hard to get back into the routine. I went to the studio twice a week but I felt no urge to take photographs or even discuss the business. It was a kind of inertia. I needed my batteries topping up and there was no way I seemed to be able to do it.

I had taken Aliki to the usual places. Down to see the White Cliffs. Stratford-upon-Avon. Edinburgh and all the usual tourist sights in London. She was interested but she didn't seem impressed. Not negatively unimpressed but like children are unimpressed. Everywhere looked exactly like the postcards and the pictures in the guidebooks. And oddly enough I wasn't impressed either. They were just places and buildings and there was a feeling of 'so what'.

Aliki was still scared stiff of London. The traffic, the speed, the hurrying crowds, were like a living purgatory for her. She never complained but her uneasiness was obvious. We had talked about living in the country instead of London and she had just wanted to leave it to me to decide.

186

At the bottom of it all I had the sneaking feeling that it wasn't just the crowds and the hassle. It was more fundamental than that. She asked questions about things. People's attitudes and customs and when I was answering the questions the answers sounded hollow even to me. I found myself excusing things that were inexcusable and explaining things that were inexplicable. She was still a fanatic about not letting taps run and wasting water. But that was understandable if you'd ever lived in primitive Africa. What I couldn't explain were much more basic things. And when I did my best to explain she would sit there looking beautiful but silent. A silence that wasn't from lack of comprehension of the facts but of the thinking behind the facts. The compulsion to own more and more things. The striving to be rich and successful. The terrible drive to be a winner. The motivations and mores of a capitalist society seemed suddenly quite incredible. I didn't try to justify them, just explain them. But I was conscious of the fact that the explanation sounded grim and hollow. It was a bit like persuading someone that putting your hand in the mincer was a good thing.

I had been at the studio that morning and I decided that I'd walk back to Chelsea but the pain in my leg made me take a rest on a bench in Hyde Park. There had been a paragraph in the morning paper about the Somalis taking another clobbering from the Ethiopians and it brought back all my anger at Shapiro and the rest of them. There had been a cheque for £7,000 waiting for me at the flat. It was from the SIS fund but the printed name on the cheque was the Ministry of Defence. Shapiro had telephoned me the day after we were back and I hung up on him in the middle of his apologies.

I still hadn't forgotten that contrived hassle with Aliki at Heathrow just to make their point. There was no end to what the creeps could do if they wanted to. Nothing violent, just that your car was always being towed to the police pound, the Inland Revenue never satisfied with your tax returns and a few words dropped confidentially

187

into various ears that could make your life a small misery. They made me sick.

As I sat in the sun that day there was one other thought that had been haunting me that came floating back into my mind. It was that European arrogance again. I'd never asked her if she wanted to live in England. I'd just taken it for granted that any African would see it as a Mecca. A highly desirable Utopia. A privilege. A prize. Despite what Haji had said about his time in England and the British. I hadn't given her love for her own people and her own country even a passing thought. It had never entered my mind that it might be a sad sacrifice for her. And if I was honest what did I myself get out of London? Who wanted friends like Shapiro and countrymen like Logan Peers? Not me. And suddenly I knew what to do. As I stood up the sun came out again as if the good Lord was giving me a pat on the back for at last recognizing the obvious. At the gate of the park I waved down a taxi and went back to the studio.

When I asked her if she'd like us to go back to Mogadishu I knew from her face that I'd made the right decision. The relief was unmistakable.

'But what about your studio?'

'I sold it this afternoon to Hugo. Part cash, part monthly payments for the next fifteen years. Far more than we'll actually need.'

'And what will you do?'

'I'm going to do a beautiful coffee-table photographic book on Somalia. The people, the country, the wildlife and the beautiful girls.'

She smiled. 'It's strange, but when I talked with Haji about you he said you were typically Somali and not European, and I'd thought that too. Maybe we were right.' She put her hand on mine. 'Are you sure, Johnny? Really sure? It's not *just* for me?'

'I'm sure, honey. How about we take the villa that

Haji found for us and buy the land at the back and grow olives and oranges?'

We got married at Chelsea Registrar's Office and were back in Mogadishu ten days later.

20

We weren't able to buy the Villa dei Fiori but we bought one on the edge of town.

The Ethiopians and the Cubans eventually stopped at the borders after they had killed roughly thirty-five thousand Somalis. The Eritrean guerrillas are still fighting the Ethiopians in the mountains north of Asmara, and winning more often than losing.

Neither Britain nor the United States lifted a finger to help the Somalis apart from some emergency food supplies from the US. Both governments will watch the Russians consolidating their hold on Addis and the Red Sea and before too long Americans will be flying into Mogadishu by the planeload, offering to build ports and airfields and make dollars available by the billion. And they'll be amazed when the Somalis doubt their good intentions. Meantime, out in the Ogaden desert and the wild scrubland of Somalia the tribes with their camels still follow the rain. They know every termite hill and dried up *wadi* for hundreds of miles but they've never heard of frontiers. They are the sons of Abraham and this is their land.

Sometimes when I look towards the sea from my workroom at the top of the villa I miss England in a way. I'm not sure what it is that I miss. It's not roses and country houses. Bougainvillaea, hibiscus, mimosa and jacaranda are just as beautiful, and they grow like giant weeds around our patio. And the calm quietness of our days and nights more than make up for country lawns. And it's not people. None was that special, and it's

190

wonderful not having to talk about the weather, the postal service, the railways and the state of the Stock Market. I miss the little creeks around Chichester and the sounds of a distant cricket match. I miss seeing the last night of the Proms on TV, and there are times when I'd like to hear the Elgar Cello Concerto actually played, not just recorded. I listen to the World Service on my short-wave receiver most evenings. I read no newspapers or magazines but I get monthly parcels of books from Hatchards. What I miss, if I do miss anything, can't be described. It isn't tangible or even real. It's somewhere between hearing Delius's 'Walk to the Paradise Garden' and the tattered paperback edition of Palgrave that's lying this moment on the top of my small writing desk.

As I look out of my window now I can see those orange trees that we wanted. There's acres of them. Barely profitable because I have to pay so much to irrigate them, but walking out in the cool blue morning to pick an orange off your own orange tree is profit enough. I had a letter about six months ago from Joe Shapiro saying how glad he was to hear that all had turned out so well for us and I was sorely tempted to reply.

I can see Haji now, sitting by the pool talking to Aliki who's smiling at something he's saying. He's married now and a politician. The plump little girl cuddling the cat is our daughter Rebecca. They're all looking up at my window so I'd better go down and join them.

PS
Remember. If you ever get tired of London there's a plane from Rome comes in every day, and the Croce del Sud still serves wonderful sorbets and raspberries . . .
Goodbye, God bless, *salaam aleikum*.